Spooky Action
at a Distance
and Other Stories

For AJ and Josie.
With love and thanks.

Acknowledgments

"The Straightened Arrow" appeared in *Ascent*
"Rot and Squalor" appeared in *Ascent*
"Here, There, Yonder" appeared in *Laurel Review*
"Everything but Bone" appeared in *Image*
"Love Canal" appeared in *Elixir*
"The Daredevil's Wife" appeared in *Eureka Literary Magazine*
"Greeting Phantom" appeared in *Mid-American Review*

Spooky Action at a Distance

and Other Stories

Tom Noyes

Dufour Editions

First published in the United States of America, 2008
by Dufour Editions Inc., Chester Springs, Pennsylvania 19425

ISBN 978-0-8023-1346-1

Cover image by AJ Noyes (charcoal and watercolor)

Library of Congress Cataloging-in-Publication Data

Noyes, Tom, 1969-
    Spooky action at a distance and other stories / Tom Noyes.
       p. cm.
    ISBN-13: 978-0-8023-1346-1 (pbk.)
    ISBN-10: 0-8023-1346-9 (pbk.)
    I. Title.
    PS3614.O98S76 2008
    813'.6--dc22

                                                        2007037407

Printed and bound in the United States of America

Contents

THE STRAIGHTENED ARROW

The Ten Commandments monument banished from
Alabama's state judicial building began a national tour
on the back of a flatbed Saturday.
                                    —*Associated Press, 8/1/04*

"Says you," I say, downshifting to take the exit. "Thus
sayeth Vance."

"Not just me," Vance says. "Thus sayeth the Apostle
John. Thus sayeth the Alpha as well as the Omega."

As we roll into Terre Haute, Indiana, Vance and I
deliberate the subject of hell. In short, I'm against it, he's
for it. Since pulling out of Montgomery three weeks ago,
we've been arguing to eat up the miles. Vance introduces a
theological topic, brushes me up on the basics, describes
his position, and then it's up to me to raise questions, poke
holes. Vance says if I ever get sick of driving truck, I could
get advocate work with the Devil.

En route to our first stop in Decatur, Georgia, we batted
around the concept of free will. Crossing Tennessee, from
Gatlinburg to Clarksville, we tackled baptism, the immer-
sion versus sprinkling debate. Last week, just outside Henderson, Kentucky, Vance introduced eternal security into
the mix, and things got heated for the first time. Vance
interrupted me to brandish the verse about no one being

able to pluck us from our Heavenly Father's hand, and I interrupted him right back with something I remembered from one of Pastor Jeffers's sermons, the notion of God spewing us out of his mouth if we taste lukewarm. "Like mouthwash," I said. "Like so much tobacco juice." Vance raised his voice to call me dull-witted and vulgar, and in response I lowered my fist on the dashboard, accidentally swerving us into the passing lane and forcing a Nissan Sentra into the rumble strips.

Once I got us righted, Vance and I decided it best to call a truce, agree to disagree and take a break for the rest of the day. Vance took it upon himself to tune in talk radio, and we cooled off by listening to other people tangle about worldly issues like campaign finance reform, tax breaks for companies shipping American jobs overseas, and war. "Catharsis," Vance said after a while, and I caught his drift.

The grind of the tour and the increasing fervency of our exchanges are beginning to wear on me. In the aftermath of a discussion, I can't tell if my faith is blooming or withering. Vance tells me not to become disheartened, that untested faith is no faith at all. He may be right, but too often his words, even when meant to encourage, strike me as holier-than-thou, and I admit to having the urge sometimes to make like Cain – hit Vance hard enough to kill him and then tell God he just died. That my wife, Misty, and I are long distance and going through a rough patch right now doesn't help lighten my mood.

Terre Haute is the midway point of the 2004 Ten Commandments Tour. The order to remove the monument from the courthouse in Montgomery wasn't even a week old when a group of local clergy and politicians began putting together the itinerary. We're not drawing the crowds originally hoped for, but the people who do turn out are enthusiastic, and despite my being no kind of a salesman, the merchandise is moving, especially the t-shirts, which have a snazzy depiction of the monument framed by lightening bolts on the back, and the tour motto – "Etched in Stone: From Moses to Montgomery" – emblazoned on the front. We also have "Basking in the Son" sun-visors, "Living Water" water bottles, "I Appeal to the Supremest Court" bumper stickers, and free brochures which offer a scripturally-based critique of the court decision and warn of the dark days ahead if America continues as is.

Vance and I luck out by catching a green light off the exit, and it's mid-day on the dot as we merge onto Third Street. Bob Evans's parking lot is jammed, as is Denny's, as is IHOP's, as is Cracker Barrel's, so we decide to get set up at the venue before eating. I haven't lately had much of an appetite anyway.

"High ground," Vance says. He smiles and opens his notebook. "Terre Haute translated. We're taking the high ground." Vance is a writer for *21st Century Christian,* a monthly magazine for and about "Godly men and women living in the Last Days." He's riding along with me as part of a story assignment. Provided he's not preempted by the Rapture, Vance sees a cover feature in his near future. I was worried for a while about how I'd come off in the story, but not anymore. At a rest stop a few days ago, my curiosity got the best of me, and I thumbed through Vance's notebook while he was powdering his nose. My name isn't mentioned once. Not a jot nor a tittle.

"Land of Larry Bird," I say, thinking I'm talking to myself. To this point in the tour, Vance hasn't struck me as much of a sports fan, talking over the baseball scores on the radio the way he does.

"Right, Bird went to college in Terre Haute," Vance says without looking up, "but he hails originally from a town south of here. French Lick."

"That's borderline disgusting," I say.

Vance nods as he closes his notebook, pockets his pen. "Downright lascivious."

I'm not entirely convinced this job's for me, yet here I am doing it. I had an inkling of this doubt from the start, but it didn't stop me six weeks ago from answering Pastor Jeffers's altar call. That Misty was sitting next to me in the pew praying I'd open my heart to the challenge was no doubt a factor – she'd whispered her petition aloud – but it wasn't only about pleasing Misty. I'd been going stir crazy in Montgomery since my layoff – I'd reacquainted myself with some old companions and habits I'd been better off without – and I thought maybe this job, minimum wage and all, was something that could help me. Keep me on the straight and narrow.

There's not to be any peeking during altar calls, but in reality, there's all sorts of peeking – I'm a peeker myself – so when I rose from the pew to make my way to Reverend Jeffers, there were a lot of amens. Seems a large portion of the congregation had been praying along with Misty, and I'd be remiss if I didn't mention how cared for this made me feel. I relish being on the minds of others, and I enjoy pleasing people, especially women and the elderly.

Later in his office, Pastor Jeffers mopped the back of his neck with his handkerchief and motioned for me to sit across the desk from him. The last time I'd been in Pastor Jeffers' office was three years before when Misty and I had gone through his pre-marital counseling program, a requirement if you want him to preside over your union. I don't remember much of what was said in those sessions, but I do recall that his eyes were on Misty most of the time, and I couldn't help but feel he was worried for her right up through D-Day.

On this afternoon, though, when it was just the two of us, Pastor Jeffers was all smiles. "It's a wonderful blessing to receive God's calling, Dusty," he said. "Lord doesn't make mistakes. He's prepared you for this."

"I've some time on my hands," I said.

"The driver we'd originally lined up is full of gall stones. Just got word yesterday. This has put us in a bind as the tour's slated to kick off tomorrow."

"Tomorrow?" I said as Pastor Jeffers opened a drawer and took out a box of cinnamon Tic-Tacs. He shook a bunch into his mouth and commenced chewing like they were peanuts. "Did you mention that from the pulpit?" I said. "I haven't yet sat down with my wife about this. I have a doctor's appointment coming up. Misty's car is past due for an oil change. Any chance I might get a week or two to tie up loose ends?"

Pastor Jeffers' forehead wrinkled as I spoke. When I finished he tilted his head back and poured a second mouthful of Tic-Tacs. He studied me as he chewed, filling the gap in conversation by shaking the now half-empty box like a baby rattle. Finally, suddenly, he poked the air with his finger as if to make room for his words. "A man asked Jesus if, before following Him, he might return home once more to say goodbye to his family. You know what Jesus said, Dusty? 'No one who puts his hand to the plow and looks back is fit for service in the kingdom of God.'"

"That's rough," I said. "If it weren't Christ, I'd consider it borderline unreasonable."

"You're better off than that guy, though, Dusty," Pastor Jeffers said. "The Lord doesn't need you until 5:30 tomorrow morning."

"I've always been lucky just like that," I said.

Pastor Jeffers shook his head. "No room for luck, Dusty. You're a key component in God's plan for national revival. Golden calves are being worshipped all over this country, and someone's got to lay down the good and perfect law. You're Moses with a flatbed, delivering to America the one true God's instructions and expectations. I'm half glad the dark powers ordered the monument removed. Why? Publicity. Airtime. God uses even the wicked to further his purposes. Poor saps don't even realize." Pastor Jeffers dropped the box of Tic-Tacs in his shirt pocket and leaned forward, rested his elbows on the desk. "On a more personal note, Dusty, I'm glad for your sake. Glad my prayers for you have been answered. There are stragglers in every flock, but no not one that the Lord can't reach, no not one that He can't bring back to His fold."

Pastor Jeffers opened his hand then as if he were the Lord reaching for me, and he kept it open, like he was waiting for a response. I thought about shaking it, but it wasn't extended out to me sideways; rather, it was straight up and down, hovering over the desk, like the man wanted me to play Mercy, that game where you and your opponent bend each other's fingers until one of you surrenders. I couldn't imagine this was what he intended, though, and a high-five seemed just as inappropriate, so I went with instinct and mirrored him, raised my flat hand over my shoulder as if my blinker were out and my intention was a right turn.

Pastor Jeffers looked confused before dropping his hand to scratch his eyebrow. My guess is it didn't even itch. "By the way, Dusty, your license is up to date, right?"

"Had it renewed just before my layoff," I said.

Pastor Jeffers smiled and raised both fists to his ears as if he'd just beaten somebody at something. "All things work together for good," he said. "Ain't no denying."

The venue in Terre Haute is a picnic shelter in the city's riverfront park. The Commandments are a dual attraction this weekend along with the 9th Annual World Hovercraft Racing Championships. Vance and I saw a billboard for the event just off the exit. Neither of us knows exactly what a hovercraft is, but I like gasoline engines as much as the next guy and am hoping to catch a race or two.

As we turn into the park, we see a few of the machines on trailers. They have giant fans on the back like those alligator hunting boats in the Everglades, but they're sleek and shiny, and the driver's seat is sunk into the body like an Indy car or an Olympic bobsled. All the guys scrambling around the machines look like their business is serious. Most are wearing coveralls, wrap-around sunglasses, and baseball caps. As Vance, the Commandments and I rumble past, not one of them looks up.

At Picnic Shelter #11, there's nothing but a posterboard and magic marker sign that reads "Ten Commandments." Some towns have crews meet us to unload the monument onto a platform or stage, but in towns like Terre Haute, crews weren't assembled for whatever reason, so the monument stays on the truck. I prefer these venues because there's less work. Besides setting up the merchandise table – I can do this in under fifteen minutes – all I have to do is take the tarp off the monument and lower the ramp so people can climb up to get their close looks. I can easily do all this in the morning just prior to show time, so Vance and I have the rest of this afternoon and tonight for ourselves.

The two of us are circling each other in the grass, stretching our legs and discussing whether to drive or hoof it back toward the restaurants and motels when a hovercraft comes into view, skimming along the middle of the Wabash River like a big dragonfly. I take my eyes off it for a second to gauge Vance's response, and in the very same moment I look back at the water, the machine flips onto its side and spins to a stop. We can't see the driver's seat from where we stand, so we're worried and start toward the bank. We're only about halfway there, though, when we spot him coming around the side of the wreck, dog-paddling crosswise against the current. When he's close enough to shore that he can walk, he uses his hands to wrestle off his helmet and flings it wildly toward shore, but it falls well short and sinks slowly in the muddy water.

A couple other men coming from downriver reach the bank ahead of Vance and me. One's in mechanic's duds, and the other's in an Oxford and khakis, like a bank teller. When the driver gets close enough to shore, the mechanic extends a hand. The bank teller, though, picks up a big stick and takes an uppercut swing at the driver's head. The blow doesn't land, but the driver's mad just the same, and as soon as his feet are on dry land, he picks up a rock. The two are squared off now, stick against rock, telling each other their intentions, but I can tell by their gabbing that neither of them is going to go through with anything, so it's not difficult for the mechanic, along with Vance and me when we arrive, to break it up. The mechanic grabs the bank teller by the shoulders, steering him away from the river and toward the parking area, so the soggy driver is left to Vance and me. He smells like rot, and his face is as red as a cinnamon Tic-Tac. He's blinking fast as if to keep tears from coming, and my guess is that the purpose of the grunting noise he's making on the exhale is to keep a sadder, more painful noise from rising.

"Hit me with a stick?" he says. "Don't think so."

"People lose their tempers, right?" Vance says. He has a handful of the guy's driving suit in one hand, and with the other he's clapping the guy on the back like they're chums. "Your friend's probably already feeling bad."

"If that guy's your friend, pickings must be slim where you're from," I say.

Vance gives me a look that makes me want to hit him with a stick, and the driver turns to face me. "You from a place where friends don't quarrel?" he says.

"We're all too busy dating each other's wives and beating each other's kids," I say. I've spent some time on both sides of the bar, have seen my share of brawls. The best way to cool a hot head is jokes. Humor reminds people that the world goes on.

When what I said sinks in, the guy smirks, and his body loosens. He looks at his muddy hands and stoops to wipe them on the grass. "Skinner's got every right to be mad," the driver says. "I'm not happy, either. What I take offense at is the stick."

"What happened?" I say, nodding to the river and his stranded machine.

"Tree limb," he says. "It's a mess out there. Absolutely unacceptable. The site's supposed to be clear. Imagine a

NASCAR driver hitting a pothole on a practice lap. Heads would roll."

"Why'd your friend take it so hard?" Vance says.

"Craft's his," the driver says. "Owner and sponsor." He looks once more at the hovercraft and then turns his back to the river. "This is the third mishap this season. Not one of them my fault, though. Not all my fault. Run of bad luck."

"He'll cool down, and the two of you will talk it out," Vance says.

"In the meantime, have lunch with us," I say. "Even the unlucky have to eat."

The driver shrugs. "Might as well. Besides, if I'm not fired, I quit."

My last night in Montgomery with Misty was unforgettable. God and I had joined forces to answer her prayer, and she was appreciative and satisfied. 'Tis better to give than to receive. That one didn't make the Top Ten, but it should've.

What was between Misty and me that night makes what's been going on since I left all the more puzzling. It's to the point now where she's got Caller ID, and if it's long distance, she doesn't pick up. I can't even leave a message as she's disconnected our answering machine. I learned all this from Pastor Jeffers, who I contacted, thinking he owed me in a way. When I asked him to talk to Misty for me, though, he turned it around and started counseling me, saying I needed to give Misty time and space. He said she'd been going through a time of transition since I left, discovering and exploring aspects of herself she'd never known. He told me that he was helping her work through it, that I needed to be patient in allowing them to discern God's perfect plan for her.

"I hope God didn't get me out of town so that He could get between my wife and me." The moment I said this was the same moment that the suspicion first occurred to me, so I was surprised by my own words.

"You're not thinking about this rightmindedly, Dusty," Pastor Jeffers said. "You're holding your own desires most dear."

"I'm human," I said. "You cut me, I bleed."

I tell this tale at lunch to Vance and Raymond, the hovercraft driver. From the river we'd taken a cab to an Irish bar that the driver recommended. The three of us ordered Reubens, and Raymond and I are drinking beer. They have a local brew on tap called Champagne Velvet, and its name alone makes Raymond and me want to keep toasting each other. I can tell that Vance is surprised by the beer — I've stuck to Diet Coke and iced tea to this point in the tour — and I sense he's taken aback, maybe even hurt, that now, in the presence of a stranger, is the first he's hearing of my troubles with Misty.

"We all bleed," Raymond says, nodding. "If Skinner would've landed that stick, I would've bled like a sonofabitch."

Vance is done eating, sitting back in his seat, wringing a napkin. Raymond and I are only about half done with our sandwiches because we've been talking and working our way through a couple three pitchers. I can tell the two of us see the world similarly, and we're mutually glad to have stumbled onto each other. If Vance is feeling like a third wheel, maybe he should write about that in his damn notebook.

"What you fellows told me in the cab about the Ten Commandments? How that judge wasn't allowed to have them in his courthouse? That's not right," Raymond says. "Doesn't strike me as fair and balanced. It goes against the Declaration of Independence, the part about the government minding its own business."

"I suppose the Supreme Court thought the courthouse was their business," I say.

"Well, that's true. That complicates the situation, them thinking it was their business. If they could make the case that they were in fact minding their own business, things could swing in their favor," Raymond says. When he drinks his beer, he curls his hand to hold the glass from behind, like a sneaky hug.

Vance squeezes his napkin into a ball and drops it on the table. "They minded their own business, but they did so unjustly. They minded their own business in such a way as to infringe upon the freedoms of speech and religion. Yours and mine."

"Of course, their argument is they're protecting those freedoms," I say, falling into rhythm. "Not everyone who walks into that courthouse is Christian or Jew."

"Let's not bring race into this now," Raymond says in a whisper that's somehow louder than his normal voice. He jerks his head to the left so we'll take note of the Asian customer at the bar. The guy's in a suit, eating a Cobb salad, talking English on his cell.

"It comes down to this," Vance says. "You can't serve both God and mammon."

"Mammons have hair and suckle their babies," Raymond says. "Except for the platypus, who lays eggs and has a beak."

"To platypussies," I say, raising my glass.

"It's platypuses," Vance says. "Or maybe platypi."

"To every single one of the freaky-looking bastards," Raymond says. Our glasses clink.

"I guess it's about that time," Vance says as he stands. "I'm going back to the truck to get my bag before checking into a motel. I think you should come with me, Dusty." He looks from me to the pitcher of beer and then back at me, slowly, dramatically, like we're in a movie, like this is some staged moment of truth.

"You go," I say. "I'm visiting with my new friend."

"Do not be given over to strong drink," Vance says. He says it like I made him say it.

"Take a little for your stomach," I say, paraphrasing the verse my father used to quote to my mother. "If it still hurts, take a little more."

"Ouch," Raymond says as he reaches for the pitcher. He laughs as he pours but doesn't spill a drop.

Vance opens his wallet, drops too much money on the table and walks out.

"My world just brightened," Raymond says. "Brother was bringing me down."

"I'm disappointing to him," I say to Raymond.

"Everybody's disappointing to somebody," Raymond says. "And some are disappointing to everybody."

Raymond and I spend the rest of the afternoon at the bar. When the after-work crowd starts drifting in, things get friendly, and by the end of happy hour, I'm fielding questions about the Commandments, and Raymond's holding forth on the ins and outs of hovercraft racing.

"They're not the original Commandments, are they?" The woman's dressed in her Sunday-best, heavily perfumed, wearing a corsage. She could be AWOL from a wedding.

"They're not Moses' stone tablets, but the words are the same," I say. "If not the actual words, the ideas, anyway. Summarized, for sure. In English, of course."

My answer seems to disappoint her, and she turns to Raymond. "Why not race cars?" she asks, poking him in the chest. "Why not boats?"

"Why not magic carpets?" I say to her loudly, but I'm not quite sure what I'm getting at.

"The firmament," says a pink-headed man in a corduroy sport coat. "That's where truth resides. That hazy border between heaven and earth. You race in the firmament."

"Professor at the university," the fancy woman says to Raymond. "Mr. Philosophical Poet after a few. Mr. Quirky Genius."

"I like it," Raymond says. "Me on my cushion of air, racing for truth in the affirmative."

"Firmament," the professor says.

Raymond turns to me. "Not just me, Dusty. You and Misty are in the affirmative, too. Not quite together, not

quite apart. You're in between, looking for the truth about
your love."

Hearing this, I'm filled simultaneously with fear and
hope, and I begin to weep for the first time as a full-grown
man. I see now that Misty and I are on the verge of catching a submerged tree limb and crashing, so to speak, but
maybe with some in-the-nick-of-time help, we could still
find a way to rise above it, so to speak, and continue gen-
tly, merrily down the stream of our love, so to speak.

"There there," the fancy woman says. She's looking at
me but squeezing Raymond's arm, like he's the one in
need of comfort. "The heart wants what it wants."

"You'll get through to her, Dusty," Raymond says.
"You'll find a way."

And then it hits me. It doesn't come from within like a
memory or an idea, but from without, like I imagine reve-
lation must. I force the words through my tears. "Misty has
e-mail at work."

"You can get on-line at the university library," the professor says. "Control-Alt-Delete will bring up the start
screen, then you log in as 'guest.'"

"What the hell are you telling me?" I say.

"Whoever's behind the counter can assist you," the
professor says. "Despite their pained expressions, that's
what they're there for."

"When it comes to computers, I tend toward distrust
and suspicion, but these are drastic times," I say to Raymond.

"Do you have an account?" he asks.

"Not that I'm aware of," I say.

"You'll use my Hotmail," he says. "Do you know her
address?"

"Haven't the foggiest," I say. "My own wife."

"There are ways," Raymond says, pushing himself back
from the table. "Let's go. First things first, though. If we're
going to a college, we need gum or mints. We're going to
be around impressionable young Americans."

"Got you covered," the fancy woman says to Raymond. She digs through her purse, comes up with an unopened pack of Wint-O-Green Lifesavers, and then holds them beside her mouth as she talks, like a commercial. "If you let me know where you're staying, I could swing by later tonight to pick up what you don't eat," she says.

"She's a saint who provides for strangers in need," Raymond says as he accepts with both hands the LifeSavers and pen the woman gives him.

"Write on this," the woman says, sliding a napkin toward him over the table. "Write neatly."

Raymond and I get directions from the professor and step into the evening's soft sunshine. After a block or two we're talking at normal volume again, and the sweat we're working up is leveling us off. Raymond's letting me bounce ideas off him of what I might write to Misty, and so far he likes them all.

"I've seen things on this tour that I could share with her," I tell him. "A vanful of cripples traveled all the way from North Carolina to see the monument when we were in Georgia. They lined up their wheelchairs in single-file to touch it one at a time. The last of them, an old woman wearing cataract sunglasses, told me a canker sore on her bottom gum went numb the moment her fingers touched the Commandments, and she thanked me as if I'd had something to do with it. In Tennessee a rabbi blessed me when I wasn't looking and then told me about King David's bodyguard, a Gentile who hosted the Ark of the Covenant for a few weeks and then enjoyed blessings the rest of his life. 'Yahweh's a good tipper,' the rabbi said. A week later at a county fair in Kentucky, a local youth pastor equipped with guitar set up in front of the monument and performed a song he'd written putting the Commandments to music. The chorus was catchy. 'Living as a straightened arrow on the straight and narrow.' The applause was thunderous.

Afterwards, the rumor around the fairgrounds was that a talent scout from Nashville tracked the boy down at the 4-H livestock pens and signed him then and there."

"Tell her everything," Raymond says. "Bring out all the tricks."

"Whatever her doubts and concerns may be, they are about the Dusty who left, not the Dusty who longs to return," I say. "I'm just now realizing this very thing."

"She'll eat it up," Raymond says.

"I don't type," I say. "I hunt and peck."

"I'm lightning on a keyboard," Raymond says. "My fingers are your fingers."

When we hit 7th Street where we're to take a right, we have to stop to wait for the light to change, and I notice an historical marker just a few feet from where we're standing. Turns out the intersection was at one time considered the Crossroads of America. Routes 40 and 63 were big in their day. Sea to shining sea, the Great Lakes to Mexico, and for the second time in an hour, I'm on the verge of tears. It hits me suddenly how big America is, how long and lonely its stretches of blacktop are, and I think of my life on the road, all the years I've spent driving rig, all the people I've passed and all who've passed me, and my chest feels full like it did back at the bar, and I have to bring my fist to my mouth and cough into it to keep myself together.

"We're on our way to making things better," Raymond says in my ear. He puts his arm around my shoulder and squeezes.

The Lifesavers have worked. His breath is pleasant and fresh, and I can only assume mine smells similarly. This instills some hope in me, and when the light changes, we cross.

Once inside the library, Raymond takes control. In no time he has us up and running on a computer, he's found

Misty's address, and his hands are poised over the keyboard, waiting for me to begin. Things are moving fast, and I feel pressure. "I know approximately what needs to be said, but I don't know what words to use," I say. "I wonder if sending the wrong message might be worse than sending no message at all."

The section of the library we're in is wall-to-wall computers, but as for people, the room's nearly empty. Besides Raymond and me, there's only the guy behind the main desk. He doesn't look like a librarian, not what I imagine a librarian to look like. He's spent some time in the weight room – he's wearing a tight black t-shirt – his head's shaved, and he's got a hoop earring in each ear. Mr. Clean is who I'm thinking.

I'm still tongue-tied when a girl walks in the room and sits at a computer down the row from Raymond and me. Upon seeing her, Mr. Clean springs into action. He's on her before her fingers hit the keyboard.

"No beverages at the computers," he says.

"Has a top on it," the girl says, holding up the cup. She's wearing a handkerchief on her head, the kind stage-coach robbers hide behind, and dangly bracelets that jingle when she moves her hands.

"Rules are rules are rules," Mr. Clean says.

The girl gets up, marches over to a wastebasket and drops in her full cup. "Happy?" she asks.

"Not especially, no," Mr. Clean says on the way back to his desk.

When the girl sits down again, she sees Raymond and me looking at her. "Whose side are you on?" she says. "As impartial observers, tell me who's in the right."

Raymond turns in his seat, clears his throat. "Tough call," he says. "Brother's just doing his job. You're just thirsty."

"Maybe you're both wrong," I say. "Maybe you shouldn't be so quick to think rules don't apply to you. Maybe he needs to learn not to sweat the small stuff."

"Do you guys go to school here? Are you like nontraditional students?" The girl's moved a few chairs closer now, and I can see she has a small jewel in her left nostril. It's hard not to stare at it.

"We're just passing through," Raymond says. "Strangers on a mission."

"What's your mission?" the girl says.

"Actually," Raymond says, and then pauses to look at me. I shrug. "It might be something you could help us with," he says.

"You being a woman," I say. "Same as my wife."

"This is Dusty," Raymond says. "He and his better half have come to a crisis point. Long story short, here we sit in front of a blank screen, looking to compose a few lines that might help initiate the healing process."

The girl gets out of her chair to stand behind Raymond and me. She leans forward as she eyes the screen, one hand on the back of Raymond's chair, one hand on the back of mine. "Don't start with 'Dear,'" she says. "Everyone starts with 'Dear.'"

When she was sitting farther away, I could've sworn the stud in her nose was red, but now, from close range, I see it's more of a purple.

"If not 'Dear,' then what?" I say.

"Dearest?" Raymond says.

"Skip the formality of the greeting altogether," the girl says. "This is your wife, right? Cut through the bull. Up front and honest. Launch into it. Project urgency. Something like, 'Here's what I need to tell you,' or 'Listen up. We need to work this out.'"

"What's your major?" Raymond says.

"Undeclared," the girl says. "It's hard for me to choose because I'm good at everything. That's not me being cocky. It's just how it is."

"You've been a big help," I say, "and I like the earring in your nose."

The girl smiles bashfully as she runs her finger over her

nostril. "My birthstone," she says. "February's amethyst."

"No kidding," I say. "My wife, too. She's the 29th. Leap year baby."

The girl's still looking at me as she sticks one finger up her nose and lifts the amethyst off her nostril with her other hand. She puts the back on the stud and holds it out to me. "New plan," the girl says. "Type this sentence: 'I have something I can't wait to give you.' Then sign and send."

"Doesn't that sound vaguely threatening?" Raymond says.

"Does she have any reason to fear you?" the girl asks me. The hole in her nose looks like a caved-in freckle.

"Not even one," I say.

"Trust me on this," she says as she takes my hand, opens my palm, and presses the amethyst into it. "Have faith."

"I know I need that," I say.

"I feel really good," the girl says. "Like I know why I got out of bed today."

When Raymond's finished typing, he tells me to click the mouse on the Send button. When I do, the girl claps, and Raymond lets out a little whoop. This makes Mr. Clean clear his throat like he wants our attention, but when we look over, all we see is the back of his narrow, waxy head. It's unnaturally smooth and still, like a mannequin's.

On my walk back to the truck to grab my duffel, I'm alone for the first time all day. Raymond called a cab from the library to get him back to his motel room. He figured Skinner would be waiting for him to talk things over, and he knew he'd have to face that music eventually, so he figured he'd get it over with tonight so he could hit tomorrow unburdened. He invited me along, but it was a situation in which I didn't see a useful role for myself, and I felt like walking rather than riding, so we said we'd see each other tomorrow at the river. We covered all this in the library lobby where the girl had told us there was a courtesy phone. Afterwards, when we returned to the computers to say our goodbyes and thank-yous, the girl was gone. I made Mr. Clean shake his head by asking if he'd seen which way she went.

I step down off one curb, up onto another, and run my thumb over the amethyst in my shirt pocket. I feel a little guilty. I have no idea how much the thing's worth and probably shouldn't have accepted it. I wonder if this is why the girl gave Raymond and me the slip; maybe she thought I'd try to give it back to her, and it was something she didn't want to have to take back. Who knows how she'd come by it, who'd given it to her? It's possible I did her a favor by taking it off her hands, maybe even a bigger favor than the one she did me.

At the long red light at Wabash Street and Route 41, there's nothing to do but stand still and watch cars go by — it's about fifty-fifty how many have their headlights on, how many don't — and I wonder about the now-empty hole in the girl's nose, how long it would take to close up if left empty, if it would ever close up the whole way.

By the time I reach the river, I have a stitch in my side. When you spend most days sitting behind the wheel, your body gets used to being moved rather than moving itself. The pain's right above my belt. What's there? What part of my guts? Maybe it's not a walking stitch at all but gall stones, like that guy who originally was supposed to drive the Commandments. Stones passed from him to me, like a plague. I wonder how he and Vance would've gotten along. I take out of my pocket the key that would've been his key, unlock and open the door that would've been his door, and pull myself up into the seat that would've been his seat.

I let my head fall back and close my eyes for a few minutes. I'm not sleepy, but it feels good to see nothing for a while. I fold my hands over my stomach and try to relax my muscles one at a time. Misty does this at night. She used to have to take sleeping pills, but she's gotten so good at relaxing that she doesn't need them anymore. She starts at the tips of her toes and moves all the way up to her scalp. Sometimes I watch her, try to guess which part of her body's she's on. I never fall asleep first.

When I re-open my eyes, it's almost the whole way dark outside, but if I concentrate I can still see the river, like a silhouette, beyond the picnic shelter, and I wonder if Raymond's hovercraft is still out there.

It's then I notice Vance's note. A page ripped from his notebook, folded long ways like a tent, and half-hidden between the passenger seat and the console. Beside it on the seat is the key I'd given him at the start of the tour. I switch on the overhead light and read.

Vance's message to me is that he's decided to rent a car, drive back home to Grand Rapids. He thinks he has the material he needs to write his story. He thanks me for letting him tag along and promises to get me a copy of the article when it comes out. He apologizes twice, once in case he overstayed his welcome, and again if his leaving seems sudden. He closes by saying he's glad I'm his friend, that he's praying for me. Under his signature, there's a verse reference. First John 5:3.

I reach behind my seat, grab my duffel and dig around to find the pocket New Testament Pastor Jeffers gave me back when Misty and I first started going to him for premarital counseling. I told him I was quite satisfied using the pew Bible on Sundays, but he insisted, saying, "This one's for Monday through Saturday, then." As he handed it to me, I remember now, he winked at Misty, like she was the one he was doing the favor for.

At first I mess up by turning to the Gospel of John 5:3 rather than First John 5:3, and I can't figure out for the life of me what Vance is getting at. "In these lay a great multitude of sick people, blind, lame, paralyzed, waiting for the moving of the water." Who's sick? I'm sick? Raymond's sick?

People coming to the river tomorrow to see the hovercraft races and Commandments are sick? When I catch my mistake and read the verse Vance intended for me to read, though, things come clearer. "For this is the love of God, that we keep His commandments. And His commandments are not burdensome."

It's not that I think that God, through this verse, is talking directly to me, instructing me to do or not do anything specific. Rather it's that I feel freed somehow, like I've been given permission to do whatever it is I think I need to do. "His commandments aren't burdensome." Some lessons feel new, but most feel like reminders, like life is spent learning the same things over and over.

I reach the flashlight under the dash, swing my legs out of the truck, head back to the trailer, and climb up with the Commandments. I loosen the straps on the monument, hop back down and pull off the tarp.

I spotlight them one at a time. They're hard to argue with, the shalt nots and shalts alike. On the one hand, don't swear, kill, cheat, steal, lie, or get jealous; on the other hand, do respect God and your folks. They're no-brainers, really. Obvious. They almost go without saying.

The only one I'm having trouble with, the one my flashlight keeps returning to, is the second. "Thou shalt not make unto thee any graven image." It strikes me that reading this rule inscribed on a touring marble monument is akin to reading the bumper sticker Vance and I saw in line at a toll booth a few weeks back: "Bumper stickers suck." Akin to people who call themselves pro-life blowing up doctors' offices. Akin to tobacco companies beseeching kids not to smoke.

As I climb back into the cab, Pastor Jeffers' song and dance about me being chosen echoes in my head. I don't know if I believed at the time what he was saying – I don't know if he believed it himself – but it turns out he was right. I turn the key to let the engine warm up. I see fuel's getting low, but I'm not going far.

I put the rig in gear and steer it slowly around the cir-
cumference of the park, ending up at the entrance where
Vance and I first came in. Seems like a lifetime ago, and I
guess, in a way, it was.

I brake at the top of the straightaway that leads to the
boat launch, and my headlights fall on the short board-
walks on either side of the slip. I can use them as guides to
aim down the middle, a straightened arrow on the straight
and narrow, and I feel like I now know why I got out of
bed today. I rev the engine in neutral until it whines, and
then I roll down my window and throw my duffel, wallet,
belt and shoes onto the grass.

I pick up good speed down the hill, more than I
thought I would. When the truck hits the water, I'm
thrown forward so the side of my head caroms off the
steering wheel, and I'm bleeding and fuzzy-headed as I
squeeze out the window into the pitch black river. The
water's surprisingly cold – my heart and brain are drum-
ming hard enough that I can feel my eyeballs pulse – but
it's only a short wade back to the dock, so I'm not in the
river for long.

Once out of the water, I try to take care of my head
wound. At first I keep pressure on the gash with my bare
hand, but the blood's trickling through my fingers and
seeping into my eye, so I take off my shirt, roll it up, pull
the sleeves tightly around my head and knot them in the
back, like I'm Rambo or a Samurai, and then I just sit still
on the dock for a while to get my bearings. To try to stop
the world from spinning, I focus on the headlights of the
truck, glowing under the water and rippling in the current
like they're reflections of headlights, like the actual truck
with its actual headlights is hovering over the water, burn-
ing diesel in the dark, idling in the firmament.

It's a good while before the lights go out, and although
my head's not feeling much better when they do, I'm satisfied as I pull myself up and turn away from the river. It
wasn't a perfect plan, but the job got done. The trailer

didn't get as deep as I would've liked, but it looks like it tipped onto its side, so the monument's completely submerged. I imagine it probably snapped the straps and slid off into the muck.

I'm not the first caretaker of the tablets to decide enough's enough. It was Moses himself who ruined the originals. He was so frustrated by the sins of his people that he snapped, dashed the Commandments to smithereens on the rocks of Sinai. He had to hike all the way back up the mountain to God, confess what happened, ask sheepishly if the Almighty had an extra copy. I imagine it was a long hike, maybe the longest ever hiked, and I imagine as he made the climb, Moses's empty hands felt heavier to him than the slabs of rock he'd hauled on the way down.

I have ahead of me a long walk, too, and I'm still dizzy as I start back up the road, and I can't tell if my head's slowly clearing or getting cloudier, but my empty hands feel light. After locating my duffel, shoes, belt and wallet, I'm enough on the ball to duck behind a tree and get myself into dry clothes. When I untie the shirt from my head, I realize that I'm still bleeding pretty good, so I make another bandage by ripping a pair of sweat pants in half.

Patched up and dry, I sling the duffel over my shoulder and am about to leave the wet, bloody shirt in the grass when I remember the amethyst. I reach my hand into the empty pocket and then halfheartedly feel around in the grass, but I know what's true, and on the hike back to Route 41, it's hard not to mourn even though I know now's not the time to dwell on what's been lost. Keys included. I should've thought to yank them out of the ignition before abandoning the truck. At any rate, going back isn't an option at this point. At what point is it ever an option? Vance will have to face this truth when he realizes that he left before having the ending for his story. No one's fault but his own. Even if it was the Holy Spirit bidding him go, his journalistic instincts should've told him to stay.

When he catches wind of the monument's relocation, I wonder how he'll spin it, if I'll end up making it into his article after all.

As I cross a set of railroad tracks, I'm surprised and proud to find myself saying a sudden, quick prayer for Vance, that he'll seek the guidance he needs in writing the story. When I'm at it, I offer one up for Raymond, too. I first express my thanks for him, and then ask that no matter how things end up with his career, he might find peace and happiness. If the fancy woman from the bar shows up at his door tonight, my desire for the both of them is that they'll be able to find comfort and hope in one another, even if only of the non-eternal variety.

Less than a block away from Route 41, I stop to re-adjust my head-dressing. I feel a bit better when I loosen it, but after a few more steps I have blood running into my eye again, so I have to stop once more to re-tighten it. It's a hindrance but nothing I can't fight through. All I'm asking of myself is to keep putting one foot in front of the other.

The rental car places are closed until morning, of course. Besides, I'm in no shape to face someone behind a counter, in no shape to drive, and it's probably necessary I travel anonymously for a while, keep my ID in my wallet and get out of Dodge while it's still dark. When I hit the main road, I'll face the southbound traffic, show them my thumb. I'm a bit worse for wear, but if I avoid trouble, if the right drivers are sent my way, those willing and able to look beyond appearances, I don't see why I shouldn't be able to fully recuperate and reach Montgomery before Misty heads to work in the morning. Without my key, the front door's not an option, but the locks are busted on two of our four living room windows, so my entrance won't be a problem. If it's one of Misty's off Saturdays, a sleeping-in morning, I might even be there bedside to say good morning when she wakes up. At any rate, our reunion's a matter of when, not if.

I know it's not something the two of us should get into right away, but eventually I'm going to have to find an agreeable way to suggest that we take a break from church. If she balks – she might see it that she and I need church more than we ever have before, or she might tell me that I can attend Bedside Baptist if I want, but she's going to stay faithful – I'll remind her that God said where two or three are gathered in His name, there He is also. She and I make two. We're enough. Says Him. This is me thinking positively. I shalt, I shalt, I shalt.

HERE, THERE, YONDER

It's the boy's first time flying, and so far he's disappointed. Too much waiting, too many dressed-up adults reading or talking on phones – they make him feel like he should keep quiet – and nothing but news on the ceiling-mounted TV at the gate. The ribbon of words at the bottom of the screen doesn't stop rolling except for commercials.

With twenty minutes to kill before boarding, the boy asks his grandmother if he can stand by the window to watch the planes taxi in and out. Without looking up from the papers she's reading, she shakes her head no, says she'd rather have him seated beside her, to be on the safe side.

Even though the boy's in fourth grade, his second time through, he can't yet read – not really, not by himself – and he doesn't like to try, so passing the time with a book isn't an option. It's not only figuring out words that turns him off; it's how, when you read, reading is the only thing you can do. He can watch TV and play his Gameboy at the same time; he can even play his Gameboy on roller blades. Reading isn't like that. And with books he can never get comfortable. The way you have to place your hands just right so you don't cover any words, and the way new books close themselves so that you lose your place, and the page turning – it's one after the other – and unless it's a book with pictures, the pages all look the same, black on white. His grandmother's TV is black and white, and the boy gets a headache if he watches it for too long, just like if he looks at a book for too long, for, say, twenty minutes, which is how long he's supposed to practice reading each night. After dinner he sits at the kitchen table, presses a book open, and moves his eyes from left to right, top to bottom. There's no going to the bathroom allowed, no radio, and no snacks or drinks. His mother, washing the dishes with her back to him, can see his reflection in the window above the sink. If he suggests that the twenty minutes must be up by now, she says not according to the timer in her head, and she tacks on another five minutes for complaining. On the two evenings a week that his mother works a late shift and he eats dinner at his grandmother's house, his grandmother sits with him on the couch in the living room after they eat, and they read together. He sees the concern in her eyes and hears it in her voice, about how many words he doesn't know, and this sometimes makes him want to try, but he can't.

Had the boy known the trip was going to begin like this, he might've argued harder for his Gameboy. He'd played it this morning in the car, but when they arrived at the airport, his grandmother told him to leave the toy with his mother, who was dropping them off. When the boy protested, his grandmother told him that he became oblivious to the rest of the world when under the Gameboy's evil spell, and that obliviousness was not a quality she wanted in a travel companion.

"I'll get good at it when you're away," his mother had said when he handed her the Gameboy before their good-bye hug. "By the time you get back, all your high scores will be history."

Now, sitting at the gate, the boy's grandmother tells him he has two choices: he can have a conversation with her, or he can sit quietly and think interesting thoughts. She has a puzzle book for him in her purse, mazes and connect-the-dots he can do by himself, along with cross-words and word-finds she can help him with, but she says she wants to save those for the plane. When she was a girl, she says, she loved puzzle books. She also loved to watch people in public places. That's a third thing he can do. He's welcome to people-watch as long as he doesn't stare.

The boy hopes he didn't make a mistake agreeing to this trip. When his grandmother stopped by the house a few weeks ago to ask him and his mother if he could go, though, she'd already bought his ticket, so he's not sure how much of a choice he'd actually had. His grandmother had apologized to his mother for not buying her a ticket, but said she figured that getting the time off work would be a problem. "You're right. Short notice like this," the boy's mother had said. She looked at the boy when she spoke instead of at her mother. This was something the boy noticed his mother did a lot when talking to his grandmother.

In bed that night, the boy had tried but couldn't think of any good reason not to go. His grandmother treated him like a baby sometimes, but he'd get to fly in a plane, skip two days of school. And the place he was going. It sounded like somewhere he should want to take a trip to. Fargo. He remembered this the next morning when his mother woke him for school. "To go to Fargo, I'll have to go far," he said.

His mother crossed the room to raise his window shade even though it was still dark outside. "No place farther," she said.

When the boarding call finally comes, the boy's grand-mother shoulders her purse and bends to lift her carry-on package. The boy's mother had warned his grandmother that she might not be able to carry on the package because it was too big, and she also questioned how her mother would manage hauling it all over the airport – she herself had struggled getting it in and out of the car trunk that morning – but no one at check-in or security had said anything, and the boy's grandmother had been able to set the package down for most of their walk to the gate because they'd ridden a moving sidewalk. After they got off the moving sidewalk, the boy's grandmother had to stop to rest twice, but one of the stops was at the restroom, a stop, the boy's grandmother told him, she would've had to make anyway.

The boy follows his grandmother through the ticket-ripper, the jet-way, and onto the plane, where he begins to get excited, even nervous, but then things stop, and he's waiting again, stalled in the aisle, and the longer he stands there not moving, the less excited he becomes, and the more the plane begins to feel like just a parked bus. The boy leans against an empty seat, slips out of his jacket, and ties the sleeves around his waist, like a backwards apron. The boy wears his jacket like this every morning at the bus stop, even the last few mornings which have been cold enough that he can see his breath in the air and do the trick where he picks up a twig or takes a pencil out of his backpack and pretends to smoke. Everyone at his bus stop pretend-smokes on cold mornings, but he's the one who started it, and they all wear their coats tied around their waists – all the boys do – and he's the one who started this, too, and he's the one who started the game where you try to get the guy next to you by lifting up his jacket, as if his jacket were a skirt, as if the guy were a girl.

Behind the boy, the restless line of passengers stretches past the loading door and down the cold, humming jet-way. In front, his flustered grandmother attempts to wrestle her package into an overhead compartment. She can get the edge of the package to the lip of the compartment, but no farther. Four tries and she's flushed, wheezing

shallowly, like her lungs are shrinking. When the boy asks
if he can help, his grandmother tells him to hush. On the
fifth attempt, her hands slip, her arms cave, and the package crashes down on her gray, tightly permed head. Her
glasses dangle from one ear, and the strap of her white
beaded purse slides off her shoulder and catches in the
crook of her elbow.

"You OK, Grandma?" the boy says. "Want me to try?"

In response, the boy's grandmother lifts her index finger
like she needs a minute to get her breath or like he's said
something wrong. Looking past her, the boy sees a flight
attendant gliding up the aisle to assist. The smile the flight
attendant aims at his grandmother isn't fresh; it's left over
from something she heard or saw at the rear of the plane.

The package is homemade: neatly folded canvas and
squarely knotted white rope. It has no handles, its weight
is uneven, and the joint efforts of the boy's grandmother
and the flight attendant are unsynchronized. When they
lift opposite ends, the center sags, and when they both
move their hands to support the center, the abandoned
ends collapse.

In the struggle, a corner of the flight attendant's white
blouse comes untucked from her navy skirt, and over the
edge of the waistband flashes the tip of a tattoo, a bright
aqua blur of what could be a piece of a heart or a raindrop
or a fish, and the boy's surprised by his urge to see the rest
of the tattoo, and he angles his head to try to get a fuller
glimpse, but he can't, and when he looks up, he's surprised
to meet the flight attendant's eyes.

With neither hand free to retuck her blouse, the flight
attendant says something quietly through her teeth, a soft
hiss that neither the boy nor his grandmother hears
clearly, but some of the passengers seated nearby do hear,
and a few raise their eyebrows and look at the boy – red-
faced, he lowers his eyes to stare at his grandmother's
shoes, fills the pockets of his roomy jeans with his fists –
and others hide their smirks by turning back to their

magazines or laptops, or staring out their tiny windows at workers on the tarmac.

A second flight attendant, a man, emerges from the swell at the front of the plane, nudging the boy on his way past. The man's sharp, dark widow's peak reminds the boy of Dracula, and Dracula reminds the boy of his teacher from last year, his first fourth grade teacher, Mr. Benjamin, who'd dressed up as a vampire on Halloween and taught in the costume that whole day, and who'd always called on the boy to answer questions even though the boy's hand was never up, even though the boy never had the faintest idea of what the question was, let alone the right answer. It had been Mr. Benjamin's decision to hold the boy back. "It's not flunking," the teacher had told the boy and his mother in their conference. "It's a second chance to get it right." Every pen in the coffee mug on Mr. Benjamin's desk was double-capped. Red ink on one end, blue on the other. At the end of the conference, as Mr. Benjamin and the boy's mother shook hands, the boy swiped one. After dinner that evening, just before reading practice, the pen fell out of the boy's pocket right in front of his mother – he'd made sure she was looking – and rolled across the floor, under the refrigerator. She acted like she hadn't seen it. She pointed to the book on the table and told him to get cracking.

The boy watches the male flight attendant reach over the shoulder of his grandmother to jab a finger into the female flight attendant's arm. "Hey," the male flight attendant says. "Not going to fit."

"Hey?" the female flight attendant says. She pulls her arm back and touches the spot he poked.

"How'd it even get on?" the male flight attendant says. "You know how many people had to screw up for this to get on? Give it here. I'll check it."

"Please," the boy's grandmother says. "It's already been x-rayed once."

"I don't mean check it through security, ma'am," the male flight attendant says, still looking at the female flight attendant. "I mean check it to baggage. You can claim it when we land."

The boy's grandmother's mouth closes as she nods. The male flight attendant hugs the package to his chest and turns toward the front of the plane to face the line of backed-up passengers. "Coming through," he says.

The female flight attendant stares after him for a moment. She opens her mouth to speak but doesn't. She shakes her head and turns, retucking her blouse as she walks away.

The boy's grandmother settles into the window seat, the boy into the aisle seat. The deal is that he can sit by the window on their later flights if he wants, but his grandmother gets the window for this first one. She's explained to the boy that the first time she flew – she and the boy's grandfather had traveled to Florida for their tenth wedding anniversary – she'd sat by the window, and looking out of it had terrified her, and despite this, she hadn't been able to stop looking. It had taken her a long time to get over this – she's still no fan of being off the ground – so, from experience, she believes it would be best for the boy to work his way up to the window seat, to ride out at least his first flight on the aisle.

As his grandmother works in his lap and then in her own to fasten their seat belts, the boy studies the impatient faces of the other passengers as they shuffle by, and he slides his elbow into the aisle so they can't avoid bumping it.

To get up and clog traffic again isn't an option, so Ingrid tries to ignore the pressure in her bladder by concentrating on other discomforts: her stiffening fingers, the spreading ache in her lower back, the anxiety-induced canker sore sprouting on the back of her tongue. She has concerns about the logistics of airplane rest rooms, anyway.

To hold it until Minneapolis is her goal, but she's nervous she won't be able to, and even if she can, she's nervous she won't have enough time to visit the restroom before she and the boy have to catch their connecting flight to Fargo. This nervousness, of course, makes her have to go worse. She loosens her seatbelt an inch, nudges her grandson with her forearm, and asks him to reach the purse that only a moment before she'd had him tuck under the seat in front of her.

She pulls the trip itinerary from the outside pocket and unfolds it in her lap as she's already done several times today: at the breakfast table, in her daughter's car, in line at check-in, at the gate, and on the toilet in the ladies room. She'd come close to going then, but her concentration had been shoddy because she was nervous about having left the boy alone with the package.

Ingrid's daughter, upon dropping off her mother and son at the airport this morning, had said, "Thousands of people fly every day and get where they're going without incident. You'll be fine." Ingrid tended to fall silent when her daughter said empty-headed things like this, ashamed that she and Jens hadn't done a better job teaching the girl reason. Watching the girl's eyes fill as she hugged her son on the sidewalk, though — the girl had dropped them at the curb instead of following them into the terminal because she thought she'd do better giving up the boy for the long weekend if she got the goodbyes over with quickly — Ingrid had been encouraged, satisfied that the girl finally seemed to have her priorities in order.

Cleveland to Minneapolis and then Minneapolis to Fargo with a thirty-minute layover in between. They board you twenty minutes before departure time, so that leaves only ten minutes to squeeze in a visit to the restroom — Ingrid can only hope there's not a line for the stalls — and that ten-minute window, of course, depends on on-time arrival in Minneapolis. Also, it's dawned on her that there's a time change she should take into account, but she can't tell from the itinerary where the hour is picked up. This plane is supposed to take off in seven minutes, at 8:20

AM, and land in Minneapolis at 9:45 AM, but Ingrid's not sure whether that's 9:45 Eastern or 9:45 Central. Holding her bladder for eighty-five minutes is different than holding it for one hundred and forty-five minutes, and she'd like to know which clock she's up against. Not everyone's a frequent flyer. The people who draw up these itineraries should consider this. And the ink, it's so light, even wavy in places so the letters and numbers don't hold still, like her TV when it's being contrary. Not everyone's twenty-twenty. Although millions are – her daughter would remind her of this – she's not.

Ingrid would ask someone for clarification, but she hasn't spotted any good candidates. The two women across the aisle appear to be deaf and, at the moment, angry with one another. They're fluttering their hands in each other's faces, battling for space, and both have tears in their eyes. One of them, the more petite woman, appears bewildered, shocked, like she's in the middle of something she hadn't seen coming. Ingrid remembers seeing the two women at the gate sitting next to each other, calm and still. She hadn't known then that they were deaf.

Of course, Ingrid could ask a flight attendant for clarification, but neither of the two she came up against while trying to stow her package struck her as accommodating. Her daughter, it turns out, had technically been right about the package being too big to carry on, but Ingrid still thinks it could've worked out had she received the right kind of assistance. If she were a flight attendant, she'd offer help generously, consider it a function of her job to anticipate questions. Confusion is something you can see in faces. Of course, she's sure that at this moment there are scores of generous flight attendants working planes all over the world, kindly sharing information, efficiently stowing uniquely shaped luggage, and doing their professional best to ensure the comfort and peace of mind of their passengers. If Ingrid were her daughter, she's sure this notion would comfort her.

Ingrid refolds the itinerary and slides it into her purse. Rather than again bother the boy, she wedges it between her hip and armrest. She allows her head to fall back against the seat and is tempted to close her eyes, but she knows she can't let herself sleep. She needs to stay on top of her grandson – the boy can be sweet, but he's not bright, and he forgets himself – and she can't risk relaxing her bladder.

The accidents she's had in the past couple months – all three at home, thank goodness – occurred while she slept. The first two times she'd dreamed she was in bed wetting herself. The dream accompanying her third accident was different. Last week, Ingrid dreamed that Jens was still alive – not only alive but young, his hair not white but once again red-blond, his stocky body once again quick and surprising – and that he came to bed late from his workshop like he sometimes used to, and that he whispered her name as he pulled her to him, and that he made love to her.

Rather than causing Ingrid, upon waking, to long for Jens, the image of Jens's young body coupling with her old one had startled her, made her age newly and urgently apparent to her, like proof. She lay half-awake for more than an hour in the warm, damp sheets – a self-inflicted paralysis, as if with night logic she'd decided that stilling her muscles might still time – and when she finally summoned the courage to get up, strip the bed, and run a bath, she'd already decided to make the trip to Fargo to attempt to mend things with her sisters, and she already knew that her grandson should go with her.

Now, as the boy digs intently to the bottom of the seat pocket in front of him, comes up with a pair of earphones and puts them on, Ingrid listens to the voice of the male flight attendant over the intercom, smug in its half-heartedness, identify exit locations and explain the fastening of a seat belt, the securing of an oxygen mask, and she senses she's one of the only passengers on the plane paying attention, senses she's one of the only passengers paying attention anywhere, on any preparing-for-takeoff plane, and she wonders what this says about her, and what it says about all those whose minds are elsewhere.

Ingrid last flew nine years ago, when she left Fargo for Cleveland the week after Jens's funeral, a month before the birth of her grandson. Her daughter hadn't been able to fly to the funeral because of the pregnancy – she'd been on doctor-ordered bed rest due to pre-eclampsia and early dilation – so Ingrid went to take care of her as soon as she could. According to the girl, the father of the child wasn't in the picture. From the little Ingrid had been able to glean, it seemed likely that the man was in the dark about the pregnancy; it seemed as if the girl felt she didn't know him well enough to broach such a personal subject with him. Ingrid and Jens had been disappointed about this aspect of the situation, of course. Initially, Jens had been angry, but this soon faded because, ultimately, he couldn't determine at whom his anger should be targeted, and eventually he and Ingrid both found themselves looking forward to becoming grandparents. Of all the reasons Ingrid mourned for Jens, this was one of the most painful, that he hadn't had the chance to meet the boy.

Ingrid had planned to return to Fargo after seeing her daughter through the birth and helping around the house for a few weeks, but on the day she was scheduled to fly back, an ice storm closed the airport, and the next day her daughter's car wouldn't start, and then there was confusion with the airline, and then another few weeks went by, and the boy was growing fast, gaining weight – he could empty both of his mother's breasts in under twenty minutes – and then he was able to hold his head up and then roll himself over and then sit up on his own, all way ahead of schedule, and Ingrid was to the point where she didn't want to miss anything else the boy would do ahead of schedule or otherwise.

When the boy was nine months old, Ingrid wrote her sisters a long letter – the information she had to convey was too detailed for a phone call – directing them to pack up her house, and listing what they should give away and to whom, what they should throw away, and what they should take extra care with. She wrote that she'd made arrangements with a moving crew to show up at the house exactly three weeks from the date at the top of the letter – she hoped that gave them enough time – and asked if they'd be kind enough to supervise the loading of the truck. She wrote that she'd already paid the movers with her credit card over the phone – this had made her nervous – but that she was enclosing a blank check for any other expenses they might incur. She also enclosed a picture of their grand-nephew who – "Let's face it," she wrote – looked like no one else in their family, not even his own mother.

The van showed up on schedule at the small house Ingrid had arranged to rent, only a couple blocks from her daughter's place, and her blank check was cashed for twenty-eight dollars and fifty-six cents, but she didn't hear at all from her sisters. She left messages on their answering machines thanking them, but they didn't call back. When she finally got them on the phone in person, they were polite but distant, moodless. Initially, Ingrid attributed their remoteness to the fact that they missed her as much as she missed them – they were just handling it differently – but nine years later, this still is more or less how they are when she calls. Although they dutifully send on-time birth-day cards to Ingrid and her daughter and the boy, the cards don't include notes or pictures – Ingrid's younger sister was somewhat of an artist, and in the past she'd always done doodle drawings of Jens and Ingrid and their daughter on birthday cards – and the Christmas letters Ingrid receives from them are copies of the ones they send to everyone. The salutation is always "Dear Loved Ones," and the closing is always "Warmest Holiday Wishes."

Of course, it was never her intention to stay away nine years. At first she didn't initiate a visit because she thought she should wait for her sisters to take the first step. She sensed that her move needed to sink in with them, and she trusted that they'd let her know when they were ready to see her as a visitor for the first time. After the first few years passed without even a hint of an invitation, though, Ingrid stayed away out of anger and stubbornness. She knew there was a struggle going on among the three of them, and she refused to be the one to cave. This is something she freely admitted to herself.

Last Christmas, though, something inside Ingrid collapsed, and she called her older sister's house where she knew the family was gathering for dinner with the intention of clearing the air. In her conversation with her younger sister, who'd answered the phone, she asked what was the matter, said she felt as if she were being punished by them, shut out and cut off, and her younger sister had responded that everything on their end was fine, suggested that maybe it was Ingrid's own conscience that was bothering her, and then handed the phone to the older sister. When Ingrid told her older sister that she'd done what she felt necessary, that her daughter and grandson had needed her, needed her still, her older sister said, "Of course," and then said she had to hang up because the roast was done.

This, the way they are with her now, is why Ingrid decided not to tell them that she and the boy are coming. She didn't want to hear anything in their voices that might dissuade her. Ingrid's daughter doesn't know about the surprise aspect of the trip, and wouldn't have gone along with it if she had. For this reason, her staying home is for the best. If there's a next trip, and she's able to get off work, she can go then.

When Ingrid feels the plane moving, she touches the boy's knee. "Here we go," she says. The boy grips his armrests, pushes himself back against his seat, and locks his eyes straight ahead. Ingrid smiles at him and decides to let herself close her eyes for a few minutes, just through take-off. Not long enough to fall asleep. Once in the air, she doesn't think she'll have a choice about using the toilet on the plane. Look out below.

There are probably pipes that channel the waste to a tank, and after each flight, the tank's emptied. That makes sense. She's not thrilled about her package being stowed near such a tank, but that's out of her hands. At any rate, she's glad she wrapped the gifts in newspaper before tying them up in the canvas. She imagines the looks on her sisters' faces when they unwrap them. For her older sister, the last thing Jens had made in his shop, the oak mantle-clock with the Roman numerals, and for her younger sister, one of the first things Jens had made, the pine ten-piece nativity set that Ingrid had set up on her porch for twenty-five Christmases.

Ingrid's older sister will weep in memory of Jens when she sees the clock, and Ingrid's younger sister will laugh when she opens her gift because of the three wisemen – Jens had named them Here, There, and Yonder after their hometowns, he said – and because of the sugar beet Jesus. Jens hadn't made an holy infant in the wood shop. Wisemen, shepherds, sheep, cows, and even Joseph and Mary he could handle, but he felt irreverent crafting Christ on his jigsaw, so Ingrid's youngest sister staked together three frozen sugar beets she'd found on the side of the road – sugar beets roll off trucks all over Fargo in the fall – drew a jack-o-lantern-like magic marker face on the top beet, and, unbeknownst to anyone, laid it in the manger, switching it with the plastic doll Ingrid had bought at the mall. When Ingrid returned home from church that night and looked in the manger, she'd screamed.

It was a risky joke, one that could've backfired, but it worked. Everyone, including Ingrid, laughed whenever the story was retold. Maybe the memory could work again to get the three of them past what was between them. They could retell the story to each other, or if not to each other right away, then to the boy. He could serve as a buffer, a liaison. He wouldn't know what a sugar beet is, and the three sisters would work together to describe one to him. Or they could all pile in the car and drive until they saw one lying on the road. It's the season.

They'll have other stories to tell the boy, too, of course.
Not all of them happy. Selling their parents' farm. Their
brother's truck accident. They could drive the boy to the
park, hike past the Roger Maris statue – the boy had hit
his first over-the-fence home run in little league this past
summer – and down to the water. There they could tell
him about sandbagging and dike-building, about, after all
that work, having to evacuate anyway as the Red River
continued to rise, finally breaking through and lapping
over the sandbags and dikes, turning roads into canals,
rushing across fields, invading barns and homes.

Her mother's half-submerged china cabinet. That's
what Ingrid's dreaming of as the plane pulls up its landing
gear.

As Tina wheels out the beverage cart and turns up the
aisle, she tries not to think about how Palmer's voice had
sounded over the intercom before takeoff. She knows that
if she thinks about it, she'll get even more pissed than she
already is, and her mood will affect the way she interacts
with the passengers. It's not their fault that Palmer has a
way of speaking too clearly, like he's under the impression
that whomever's he's talking to has some sort of deficiency
that he needs to make allowances for. She doesn't know if
she's bothered by this speaking-too-clearly thing only
sometimes because he only does it sometimes, or because
she's inconsistent in noticing and disliking this thing he
always does. She wonders how this question might be
linked to the question she has about whether being with
Palmer is something that's good for her or something that
she needs to find a way out of before it's too late. Whatever too late means. Maybe it's already too late. Maybe
there's no such thing.

Tina doesn't necessarily expect better treatment than
the other girls – although, would that be unreasonable? –
but she certainly doesn't expect worse. The way he'd

poked her arm, the way he was short with her, the way he was downright cold, how every on-the-job exchange between them now means doubly. That he was a prick about the old woman's package might simply mean he was irritated that Tina hadn't decided right off the bat that it needed to be checked, but it might also mean he's still pouting over her confession to him last Thursday night that before he'd asked her out for the first time, she'd thought he might be gay.

Of course, she understands this bothering him. As soon as she'd said it, she wished she hadn't, but she hadn't said it to be cruel or to humiliate him; she'd meant it almost as a compliment. Like she'd thought his being gay was too bad because otherwise he was a good prospect. Why did she think he was gay? Palmer, of course, had wanted to know, and when Tina paused before answering – she was trying to remember if she'd come to the conclusion on her own, or if someone had told her that he was gay – he interpreted her pause as stalling. "Forget it," he'd said, and the conversation had ended there. Tina knew the subject would eventually have to be revisited, probably tonight in Minneapolis – they'd made dinner and hotel reservations three weeks ago – and she's not sure she's up for it, although she suddenly has an idea about what she could tell him, that one of the reasons she thought he was gay is the way he over-pronounces words. She could actually over-pronounce her own words as she tells him this to demonstrate. Of course, this isn't true, but it would be a way for her to bring this thing that bugs her to his attention, and maybe if she linked the over-pronouncing thing with the gay thing, he'd stop doing it – he had nothing against homosexuals, he'd told her, but that didn't mean that her assumption didn't bother him – and if he stopped over-pronouncing, then there would be one less thing she would want to change about him, or at least one less trigger to remind her of the things she didn't like about him, and maybe as a result, whatever was going on between them would clarify itself. Currently, Tina felt that she disliked Palmer too much to decide whether or not she loved him.

Tina starts at the back row and works her way up. "Would you like a beverage?" She prefers the passengers who answer with an order right away – "Coke," "Bud Light," "just water" – rather than the passengers who say simply "Yes," forcing her to ask the second question, "What would you like?" as if they couldn't think that far ahead. She'd like to avoid this scenario by beginning each exchange with the question, "What can I get you to drink?" assuming that if someone doesn't want anything, they'll simply say, "Nothing," but according to the book, she can't do this. Palmer says this is because the airline wants to give passengers every opportunity to turn down complimentary services. When Tina told him that she'd heard Penny, who's been a flight attendant longer than Palmer and Tina put together, suggest to customers on more than one occasion that she get them a blanket or pillow, Palmer said that wasn't the same thing at all because blankets and pillows can be re-used. When Tina suggested that they might sell more alcohol if they led with "What can I get you?" rather than "Would you like something?" because "What can I get you?" is more like what bartenders ask, Palmer disagreed, arguing that people who drink on planes have that as their flight plan from the get-go. "People don't buy booze on impulse," he said. Tina figured he was probably right, but hated how he offered his opinion as fact.

Halfway through the plane, Tina's impressed with this group. No one's forcing her into conversation, and everyone seems to understand the basics of beverage ordering. On some flights, Tina gets the impression that she's not only dealing with first-time fliers, but also with people who've never been to a restaurant before, never been to a bar or a drive-thru window. Some things work the same in the sky as they do on the ground. This group seems to get it.

When Tina hits the row behind the boy and his grandmother, she sees the old woman is sleeping. As for the boy, he's turned toward the window, and he has headphones on. Tina reaches out and pulls them off the boy's head. This startles him. "Thirsty?" she says.

"How much?" he says.

"For you, free," Tina says, and she suddenly knows what Palmer will say tonight when she tells him about the boy's wandering eyes. He'll say, "Well, at least you can be sure he's not gay." That's how they'll get into it.

"Coke?" the boy says.

When Tina looks across the aisle and to the next row, she sees two women arguing in sign language. She guesses they're arguing. They're both upset at any rate. They hack at the air like their hands are hatchets. Tina decides to skip them, swing by later when the scene's calmed down. As a flight attendant, you have to have a feel for this. Husbands and wives, parents and kids. You don't want to get in the middle.

The curtain separating first-class and coach opens, and Palmer peeks his head through. Tina wonders if she's what he's looking for. When he spots her, she takes the opportunity to look right through him, as if he were air, as if the curtain were still closed.

The boy can't decide if the plastic-wrapped snacks he got with his Coke are crackers or cookies. They're sweet but thin and have holes on top like saltines. He has eight of them. Four packages of two. He got double because his grandmother's still asleep.

As the flight attendant moved on to the next row, the boy couldn't help looking. Nothing to see, though; everything tucked in. Heart, raindrop, fish. The glimpse he'd had was so brief. An eagle's wing, a cresting wave. It's almost better this way. A flower petal, a tongue.

Just as the boy's taking his last swallow of Coke, he sees

the male flight attendant step through the curtain, approach the tattooed flight attendant who's serving passengers a few rows in front of the boy, and say something into her shoulder. The tattooed flight attendant shrugs. If she's being asked a question, "I don't know" is her answer. The male flight attendant again talks into her shoulder – maybe something else this time, maybe the same thing – and she shrugs again. She opens a can, pours it in a cup, and offers it, smiling, to a passenger. The boy used to shrug off Mr. Benjamin. The teacher would hover over the boy's desk during tests. "Check your work," he'd whisper. "Take your time." The boy would find a spot on his paper to stare at until the man moved on.

You plug the headphones into a hole on the armrest, and under that hole are the volume and channel dials. The boy figured out all this on his own. There are five stations: two talk and three music. The talk stations are money and sports. The music stations are classical, Top-Forty countdown, and country.

The country station is all songs by the same guy. "A look back at the singing and songwriting career of Kris Kristofferson." The boy likes the name. He might have heard a couple of the songs before, but sung by different people. The boy thinks Kris sings them better. Sometimes the way Kris sings, it's almost like he's talking instead of singing, and he has a deep voice. Kris's voice is a voice the boy would like to have. Kris can sound sad and happy in the same song. He'll start off one way and end up the other, like something happens to him in the middle of singing, like he suddenly remembers or forgets something that changes the song. "Kris Kristofferson," the boy says, and then takes off his headphones so he can hear himself say it. "Kris Kristofferson."

It's hard to keep from watching the women across the aisle. When he does glance over, they don't seem to notice, but he knows if his grandmother were awake, she'd nudge him with her elbow and whisper "Not your business" loudly and wetly into his ear just like she whispers "Be still" when they're in church. But it's not like he knows what the women are saying. It's not eavesdropping. They could be swearing at each other – that's what their faces suggest – but he can't know for sure. It's just cool how fast their hands move, like karate. The boy wonders which is faster, sign language or regular. A deaf person and a regular person start at the same time, say the same thing. Who finishes first?

Last year, a lady came into the boy's school to teach the students how to say "Hi, Kyle" in sign language because they were going to have a deaf kid in their class. The kid never showed up, though. Mr. Benjamin told the class that Kyle had ended up going to another school. "Lucky him," Zach Billups had said, and the rest of the class laughed.

"Think about what you just said, Zachary," Mr. Benjamin said. "And the rest of you, think about what you're laughing at."

"I mean lucky about not having to go to this school, not about being deaf," Zach said.

"Still," Mr. Benjamin said.

The boy puts his hand under his leg, signs into the seat. "Hi, Kyle." He's pleased he remembers.

The tattooed flight attendant and male flight attendant are returning the beverage cart to the rear of the plane – the tattooed flight attendant is in the lead, walking backwards and pulling, and the male flight attendant is pushing – when they're stopped by the deaf woman in the aisle seat. "Excuse me," she says to the tattooed flight attendant. "Is it too late to get a drink?" Her voice is louder and stays in the air longer than most, and it sounds like she's talking through her nose, but what she's saying is clear enough. When the tattooed flight attendant shakes her head and smiles, the woman says, "Ginger ale, please." The boy watches the flight attendant shake her head again. She means, "We don't have ginger ale," but the deaf woman thinks she means, "I don't understand you," so she says,

"Ginger ale" again, this time more slowly and loudly. The tattooed flight attendant shakes her head yet again – this time she shrugs her shoulders, too, and the male flight attendant does the same when the deaf woman looks to him – but the deaf woman still doesn't understand. "Ginger ale!" the deaf woman says a third time. This time it's a drawn out yell. The boy notices a few passengers turn around, and he hears his grandmother grunt. He turns to see her eyes twitch, her head roll, but she stays asleep.

Before the deaf woman can say "Ginger ale" for a fourth time – it looks to the boy like she's just stopped crying and might be about to start again – the other deaf woman, the one sitting by the window, tugs her arm and signs to her. When the woman trying to order the ginger ale turns to face the tattooed flight attendant again, her eyes are closed, and she's smiling weakly. "Sprite?" she says softly, and the tattooed flight attendant nods, pulls out a cup and scoops some ice. On the other end of the cart, the male flight attendant opens a drawer and reaches for a can. They both look tired, like the boy's mother when she gets home from work. The tattooed flight attendant holds the cup over the middle of the cart while the male flight attendant pours.

When the deaf woman on the aisle gets her drink, she looks at the other deaf woman, and they both begin to laugh. By the time the flight attendants are gone, the women are laughing so hard that they're holding onto each other. They try to sign, but can't. Their arms are useless. When the one in the aisle seat notices that the boy's watching them – she doesn't stop laughing – the boy looks away, but he can't help smiling.

It's when the boy leans over his grandmother to try to see out the window that he smells something. He sniffs the seats in front of him and the air coming out of the vent above him, and for an instant he wonders if it's him, but eventually he realizes it's her. He slides his hand onto the edge of her seat, just under her skirt, between her knees, and feels the damp cushion. He knows his grandmother's awake when she takes his hand and puts it in his own lap.

"Are you OK?" the boy says. "Are you sick?"

"No," his grandmother says. She sits up and slides her fingers underneath her glasses to rub her eyes.

"You can cover yourself with my jacket," the boy says, lifting himself off his seat so he can pull it out from under him.

"Yes, OK. Thank you. That's a help." She drapes the boy's jacket over her lap and asks him to get her purse. "Listen now," she says. "When we land, we'll get off last. We'll stay in our seats until everyone else is off."

"I won't get up until you say," the boy says.

"I need you to look somewhere else now," his grandmother says, pulling some Kleenex out of her purse. "Until I tell you it's OK."

The boy turns toward the aisle. The deaf women have calmed down, but they're still smiling, wiping tears. The one who ordered the Sprite picks up the cup, takes a drink, and holds it out to the other woman. The other woman shakes her head and says something that starts them both laughing again. The one with the mouthful of Sprite cups her hand over her mouth, and her eyes get big, like she's going to lose it. They're not laughing at his grandmother, the boy decides. They don't know about her. They have their own thing.

If the boy had to give up one of his senses, and he got to pick which one, he'd choose hearing. There's signing, and you learn how to read lips. The lady who came to his class had told the kids they should say "Hi, Kyle" with their mouths even as they signed it. "I'm sorry, we don't have ginger ale." The tattooed flight attendant should've mouthed the words instead of just standing there, shaking her head and shrugging.

His grandmother hasn't yet given the OK, so the boy knows he can't turn around, but there are only so many places to look. He rests his head against the back of his seat.

He wonders what his mother's doing now, what she'll do after work today. He wonders if she's wondering about him, if she wishes she could've come along. He wonders if she's alone, if she feels alone.

The boy closes his eyes. He does this sometimes during reading sessions. His mother has caught him a few times, but if he remembers to turn pages now and then, he can usually get away with it. Sometimes he tries to focus on the colored shapes that float across the inside of his eyelids, like fish in an aquarium – he doesn't know if everyone sees these shapes when they close their eyes, or if it's just him – and other times he tries to think of nothing, of blankness. Blindness would be his second choice. You can still see with your eyes closed. In your brain. If the boy focuses on nothing hard enough, his mind will start playing movies for him. Scenes in which he wins at something or rescues someone, or memories, sometimes ones he didn't know he had.

The house and back yard that the boy pictures are not his; he doesn't know who they belong to. He's little, and he's running a toy truck along the side of a chain link fence when a train rushes by. The tracks are close, only a few yards beyond the fence, and he's startled. It doesn't seem possible that a train could sneak up on you, but this is what it feels like. He drops the truck and runs crying toward the house. He can't even hear his own crying, the train is so loud, and somehow the farther he gets from the tracks, the louder the train roars, like it's chasing him, gaining on him. When the boy finally reaches the back porch of the house, he sees his mother sitting on the lap of a man he doesn't recognize. The man is sitting on a lawn chair, shirtless, and the boy's mother is kissing the man with her eyes closed. Her hands move over the man's chest and shoulders, over his tattoos, like she's trying to feel them or wipe them off.

When the boy hugs his mother's leg, she opens her eyes and stops kissing the man. She gets down off the man's lap to kneel in front of the boy, and she covers his ears with her hands. The boy can still hear the train, but it's not so loud now. It's better now.

When the boy's grandmother tells him he can have his jacket back, that it's OK now to look, he'll pretend not to hear. He'll keep his head back, his eyes closed, and she'll smooth his hair like he's asleep.

EVERYTHING BUT BONE

Laurel's sorry for Steven's loss, says as much into his shoulder when they hug hello. "To know Charles was to love him, Steven. Truly."

Steven's nose grazes Laurel's neck, her earlobe. The soft compromise of lavender and lilac. Her bouquet, like she's a wine cork. When he and Laurel were together, Steven should've more often gone the fragrance route for birthdays and anniversaries, explored more fully the possibilities of bath oils and soaps, lotions and splashes.

Nostalgia's part of it. Steven used to be Laurel's husband. They've met at the airport to pick up their son, Oscar, who's flying home from college for the funeral of his grandfather, Steven's father. So grief's part of it, too.

"Even after you and I split, Dad always asked about you," Steven says softly into Laurel's hair. He's taking long, deep whiffs, so it's a challenge getting this out, gathering the wind.

Laurel's body feels different to Steven. He wonders if she's joined a club. It's mid-October in Buffalo, but she's going sleeveless, sporting toned arms and a light, healthy tan. Her hair's changed, too, since the last time he saw her. Short and spiky now. No fuss, fool-proof.

When they let go of each other, Laurel digs in her purse for a Kleenex, dabs her eyes. Steven looks away, taps his watch. "On time would be now," he says.

What Laurel says next is news to Steven. Oscar's not alone on that plane. "The girl's name is Marla," she says.

"He's bringing a date to the funeral?" Steven says. Distressed, his tendency is to pick his beard. Oscar has the same habit. A few years back, in the week before his S.A.T.'s, the boy cleared a dime-sized hole just left of his chin. Steven's father, too, pawed at his beard in uncertainty, sometimes chewed on the whiskers he plucked, like cud. From what Steven's heard of death, he knows his father's beard continues to grow even now, three days after the last heartbeat echoed through the body. From what Steven understands, hair outlasts skin and blood, outlasts muscle, beats everything but bone.

"He called to tell me just last night," Laurel says. "What could I say? Maybe he feels he needs to bring her. To get through."

"Springing this on us," Steven says. "It changes things."

While Steven and Laurel hang back – Laurel settles onto a bench between a newsstand and a Starbucks; Steven stands beside her – most of the people waiting to greet passengers bunch in front of the terminal exit. Two kids at the head of the swell hold balloons. The brother's balloon says, "WELCOME HOME," and the sister's balloon says, "MOM." Next to them, a limo driver holds a sign, but he's got it flipped. He's hugging the name to his chest like it's a secret.

"Oscar and this girl started off lab partners," Laurel says as the first wave of passengers rambles through the exit. "Within minutes of meeting, they were pricking each other's fingers. Prior to their first official date, they'd already run a battery of tests on each other's urine."

"Romantic," Steven says. "I hope this isn't too forward, but may I have your atomic number?"

"You're being Oscar," Laurel says. "You're suggesting a line he could've used on Marla in the lab." She nods. "Humor was a quality of your father's. The first time you brought me home to meet Charles he told a joke to break the ice. I wish I could remember it."

"Jokes he took seriously," Steven says. "He bought books."

"You should tell a couple of his favorites tomorrow at the service."

"Sure," Steven says. "A eulogy to bring the house down."

"Of course not," Laurel says. "That's not what I'm saying." Her voice gets thick, like she's ready to weep again. "Don't hear me like that."

"No. I know," Steven says. Laurel's turned from him now. She's got her compact out. "What you said wasn't wrong," he says.

"This is hard for you, I know," Laurel says. Her Kleenex is in a ball now, and she's turning it over in her hand, looking for a clean spot. "For all of us, though."

"You're right," Steven says. "We're all OK, though. We're fine." If Steven could find a way to brush his lips against Laurel's neck, he'd be able to preserve her essence on his moustache. He'd have it for later to fall asleep to. An olfactory lullaby.

Laurel looks past Steven, and her eyes brighten at what she sees. She waves with one hand, snaps her compact shut with the other, and stands.

When Steven turns, he's surprised by the bareness of his son's face, smooth and white as an egg, and the wisp of a girl in Capri pants who holds the boy's hand. This girl looks like Oscar. She has his small ears, his long eyelashes. She could be his sister, at least a cousin. She has his high, white forehead. Side by side, they're two blank billboards.

"You all right, Mom?" Oscar says, shifting his backpack from one shoulder to the other.

"Look at you," Laurel says. "Baby face." She reaches up to run her hand along her son's clean jawline and swallows him in a hug.

"I'm Marla," says the girl, extending to Steven the hand that Oscar's just released. She slides her fingers in and out of Steven's so quickly that he barely feels them. "I'm sorry for your loss," she says.

"Welcome," Steven says.

When Laurel releases Oscar, he steps to Steven. "Dad," Oscar says. He shakes Steven's hand with one arm and wraps the other around Steven's shoulder. Two greetings.

"You have bags to claim?" Steven asks. His son's cheeks gleam like wax fruit. Without his beard, Oscar looks more like his mom than his dad. It's not even close. Line up Oscar and Laurel next to this Marla, and any passerby would think, "Family." The older guy with the beard? Maybe their friend. Maybe their ride.

"One suitcase," Oscar says. "One between the two of us."

"Packing light," Laurel says. She keeps a hand on Marla's back as she talks. "That's a skill."

Kliessen beards come in thick and early. There are no thin spots where you can see through to pink, not even in places where some men have problems – high on the cheek, under the bottom lip – and the color's rich and full.

In his wallet, Steven has photographs of three generations: two in color, one in black and white. He's trimmed the pictures to credit card-size so they fit the plastic sleeves. They're more for himself than for others – they're not for whipping out and bragging over – but now at the baggage carousel, standing in wait with Laurel, Oscar, and Marla, Steven's tempted. One picture each. He could deal them around like cards.

In the most recent picture, Oscar plays the drums. During his junior year in high school, he and his friends formed a speed-metal band, Sprained Throat. Oscar's overgrown beard served as a prop of sorts, afforded the band stage presence. During Oscar's solos it flapped frantically like a bat in the sun. Steven once saw part of a gig incognito, tracked Oscar and his band out to Lackawanna and milled around the outskirts of the party long enough to snap a few pictures. He didn't want Oscar to see him there. He wanted to know who Oscar was when he wasn't around.

In the oldest photograph, the black and white shot, Steven's father sits outside on a log bench with a baby propped in his lap. A thick, bare tree branch hangs low to his left, and the ground's covered in leaves. Steven likes to think it's a clearing in the woods, but it could easily be someplace tamer, a park or back yard. Charles wears a turtleneck sweater and has a pipe clamped in his teeth. The baby's fists are full of Charles' beard, and Charles' expression of mock agony causes the baby's healthy cheeks to bunch into a grin. The baby's not Steven. There's a year scrawled on the back of the photograph; Steven hadn't been born yet. Steven doesn't know who this baby is. He has no brothers or sisters, no older cousins.

In the third picture, the one of Steven, it's Halloween. He wears a werewolf mask, and his beard, hanging below the collar of his t-shirt, matches perfectly the color of the mask's mane and muzzle. His hands are cocked menacingly behind his ears, his fingers bent like claws.

Steven remembers as a kid going to an elementary school party as the Tin Man; he remembers in high school greasing his hair back and sporting fangs for Dracula; and the year before they married, he remembers dressing up with Laurel as a cave couple, the club and the fur. Truth be told, though, he can't recall the werewolf. But pictures don't lie. In the background are cupboards Steven recognizes from the kitchen of Laurel's and his first apartment out on Grand Island, and he recognizes the electric jack-o-lantern glowing on the counter. He wonders if he had a good night. If there was a party, he wonders if he got carried away, drank too much, howled too often or too loudly, lifted his leg on anything.

Steven takes his wallet from his back pocket, but when Marla glances at him and smiles, he doesn't go to the pictures; instead, he leafs through the bills in the back, like there's someone he needs to tip.

When Oscar spots his suitcase on the carousel, he splits the two guys in front of him with his shoulder and an "Excuse me." One of the guys stares at Oscar's back and shakes his head like Oscar's out of line. But what would the guy have had Oscar do? Let the bag go by, wait for the next pass? Steven would like to say something. Give the guy a long, low growl. Flash some teeth. He's the only one who noticed, though, and Laurel, Oscar, and Marla are already hustling off toward the parking garage, talking restaurants. Steven's five paces behind, straining to hear. He'd like input.

Oscar's game for anything but Mexican. Steven hears "sombrero," then laughter, then "seafood."

"I'm on a seafood diet," Steven calls out.

Marla turns without breaking stride. "Whatever you see, you eat," she says.

"You're onto me," Steven says.

At the Red Lobster near the airport, Steven goes healthy, opts for the Admiral's Platter rather than Neptune's Feast. Flounder, shrimp, and scallops on both, but the former's broiled, the latter's fried. His three-page menu folds twice. The server collects it, turns, and smiles at Oscar because it's his turn now and because she believes that, even in her ponytail, apron, and standard issue white blouse and black slacks, she's cuter than the girl hugging Oscar's arm.

Laurel arrives back at the table from the rest room just as the server is leaving. She'd left her order with Steven, though. Blackened tuna, no dressing on the salad, skip the potato, substitute the steamed garden medley. "There was a line," she says. "What did I miss?"

"We ordered," Steven says. "Before that some ice cubes clinked. The booth behind us emptied."

"My turn now," Marla says, reaching under her chair for her purse. "If you'll excuse me."

"Over by the bar, Hon," Laurel says. "Under the hammock."

"I see it," Marla says. As she leaves, she smiles at Oscar who smiles back. They've got secrets. There's them, and then there's the rest of the world.

"That's not a hammock," Steven says to Laurel when Marla's out of earshot. "It's a fishing net. There's a theme at work here."

"I'd sleep in it," Laurel says. "Looks comfortable. Right above the bar. They could hand drinks up to you. What do you think, Oscar?"

"Either, but not both," Oscar says. "A fishing net would make for a stinky nap."

"Oscar would know stinky naps, wouldn't he, Steven? Remember that apartment on Grand Island? Cramped and warm. That tiny bedroom. We had to keep the crib in the hallway." Laurel leans across the table and grabs her son's wrists, like handcuffs. "It never failed. As soon as you'd fall asleep, you'd fill your diaper. Your father and I would agonize over whether to wake and change you or let you sleep. It took so much effort to get you to sleep!"

"Too bad Marlo's not here for this," Steven says. "Had she turned down the stewardess, skipped that second diet cola, she'd be getting an earful right now."

"Her name's Marla, not Marlo, Dad," Oscar says. "An 'a', not an 'o'. And what's wrong with diet cola?"

"Right," Laurel says. "Marla's softer, more feminine. It suits her. I'd also mention there's no such thing as a stewardess anymore. They're flight attendants, just like the young woman hustling over here to top off our iced teas isn't a waitress; she's a server."

"Miss, I have a question," Steven says to the girl as she arrives at the table. She's got two pitchers, iced tea and water. Both holsters full.

"All ears," she says. She moves from glass to glass and pitcher to pitcher quickly, effortlessly.

"Steven," Laurel says. "Cease and desist."

Steven continues. "Would you rather be a waitress or a server?"

"If it's all the same to you," the girl says, "let's make me a physician's assistant."

"Good answer," Steven says. "You'll go far."

Laurel's moved on. "So let's hear it, Loverboy," she says to Oscar. "How'd you meet this cutie?"

Steven remembers this about Laurel. She's most comfortable asking questions she already knows the answers to. During their marriage, Steven was sometimes annoyed by this habit, sometimes pacified. Frustrated by the senselessness of it, he nonetheless appreciated how it filled up the quiet. And he understands why she does it. Ground already covered is safe ground. The mines have been swept.

Steven would've liked to have had a few safe, pre-answered questions to ask his father over the last few weeks of his life. Early in Charles' stint at the hospital, Steven had been able to carry on conversations with him. At least they could watch a Sabres game together on the wall-mounted TV. As Charles' condition worsened, though, he didn't want the TV on because he said it distracted him – from what? Steven wondered – and he became unable to harness the breath necessary for conversation. The visits grew steadily quieter. Near the end, the silence of the warm, sterile room would hum in Steven's ears for hours after he returned home to his apartment.

The question Steven began every visit with – first thing in the door, he asked his father how he was feeling – was not a question he ever knew the answer to. Charles would go into great detail, body part by body part, and many evenings his answers seemed to surprise even himself.

Rather than taking the edge off the quietness of the room, these answers sharpened and deepened the silence that followed, and as Charles flipped through the magazines Steven had brought from the gift shop, Steven would find himself doing things like counting his father's exhalations, or staring out the window into the staff parking lot, imagining the specialty of each arrival and departure. Anesthesiologists tended to be tall and lanky, their limbs thin and flexible like plastic tubing. Male pediatricians carried a paunch; their female colleagues were heavy-breasted, wide-hipped. Heart surgeons walked deliberately, gracefully, as if hurrying across tightropes. Cancer specialists tucked newspapers and umbrellas in their armpits. ER doctors and nurses sipped coffee out of travel mugs, wore sunglasses.

"On the third date, I cooked her dinner," Oscar says, summarizing the story of himself and Marla. "And on the fourth date, I cooked her breakfast."

This makes Laurel snort in her water. Steven can't tell if the snort is authentic or staged.

"Breakfast?" Laurel says between little coughs into her fist. "How'd breakfast come about?" She touches her throat lightly when she says this, like she's trying to steady her voice from the outside. Given the go ahead, Steven would be glad to help. He'd carefully massage the length of her neck, from chin to shoulders, interrupting the process only occasionally to smell his fingers, like when he chops onions.

"How'd breakfast come about?" Oscar says. "We woke up hungry."

"We've reared a smart ass, Steven," Laurel says.

Steven hadn't called Laurel with the news of his father's death. He'd called Oscar at school, and, at Steven's request, Oscar had called Laurel. Steven regrets this now, fears he pushed off too much on his son. In hindsight, the child breaking the news of the grandparent's death to the parent seems unnatural, unhealthy. Also, Steven laments the missed opportunity to tell Laurel himself. Sitting next to her now, he wishes telling her was still his job. Steven would like to have to take her aside and find the voice. He'd like to feel those toned shoulders shiver.

Since their arrival at the restaurant, Laurel's scent has shifted. Floral to citrus. Perhaps in the restroom she'd opened a new bottle and re-sprayed or re-dabbed. Is that allowed? At any rate, she's lemon-lime now, like a see-through soft drink.

Marla gets back to the table as the salads arrive. She wasn't gone long. This server and her cronies back in the kitchen are on top of things. They know it's all about turnover.

"Around here, you order salad, you get salad, and you get salad fast," Steven says.

"That's our motto," the server says as she distributes the plates. She has anesthesiologist arms, as thin at the biceps as they are at the wrists. "And finally the soup," she says as she sets down Oscar's bowl.

"Hold on," Laurel says. "What's your motto?"

"The customer's always right," the server says as she places a basket of biscuits next to Oscar's elbow and smiles at him like they're sharing a joke. "Can I get anyone anything? No? Then I'll return soon with your entrees."

"Marla," Laurel says as the server departs, "are there Red Lobsters in Canada?"

"What am I missing?" Steven says.

"It came up earlier that Marla is Canadian," Laurel says. "You missed all sorts of interesting exchanges on the drive over, Steven. We should've had walkie-talkies so that you could've kept up in your car."

"You don't sound Canadian," Steven says as he watches Marla transfer tomato wedges from her salad bowl to Oscar's bread plate.

"Are you challenging her?" Laurel says. "Would you have her pass a test?"

"You could make her skin a moose," Oscar says through a mouthful of biscuit.

"Better yet, you could have me skin a moose in French," Marla says.

"Right," Steven says. "Very good." He takes a long swallow of iced tea. "So Canada. What do your parents do up there?"

"My mum's a trapper-trader, and my pop's a Mounty," Marla says. As she talks, she holds her fork in both hands and rubs the tines with her thumbs, like it's a good luck charm.

"Good material," Steven says. "Good delivery."

"Seriously, though," Marla says. "My father passed away a few years ago, and my mother helps run my grand-pop's shop in Guelph. Formal wear."

"I see," Steven says.

"A Mounty," Oscar says. "That was great." He's working on his bisque now, has dropped his face to within an inch of the bowl. There's barely enough room for the spoon.

"I don't mean to get carried away," Marla says. "I know it's a hard time. I'm just excited to finally meet Oscar's family. When I'm nervous, I clown."

"You're fine," Laurel says. "You're being charming."

"Levity can be good," Steven says.

"You should come home with Oscar for Thanksgiving, Marla," Laurel says. "A happier occasion."

"I'm not sure what we're doing for Thanksgiving," Oscar says.

"You might not come home?" Steven says.

"We might head to Marla's," Oscar says. "Go camping."

"You can camp anytime," Laurel says. "You should come home."

"Maybe we should, Oscar," Marla says. "I've never done American Thanksgiving. The Macy's Parade, right? We could watch that."

"Yes, we'll initiate you into all our exotic customs,"

Steven says. "You've probably never hung a Thanksgiving stocking, never embarked on a Turkey-egg hunt."

The server passes by on her way to another table, and Steven raises his almost empty glass. "Excuse me, physician's assistant," he says. "When you get a chance." The server rolls her eyes as if she's annoyed, but not really-but she could be-and nods.

"What's that about?" Marla asks.

"We like humor in this family," Steven says. "Right, Oscar? We know our way around a joke."

"That's all I was saying at the airport, Steven," Laurel says quietly. "That's all I meant."

"I know," Steven says.

"Tell me one of these jokes you know your way around," Marla says to Steven.

"You're a science type like Oscar, right?"

"Chem major," Marla says.

"I have a biology joke," Steven says. "Best I can do." He clears his throat, folds his hands in front of him on the table. "This scientist wants to do a set of experiments on the leaping ability of frogs. So he puts a frog on the floor, yells, 'Jump!' and measures. He writes 'twelve feet' in his notes. Then he rips off one of the frog's legs, yells, 'Jump!' and writes 'eight feet' in his notes."

"A joke from the dismemberment genre," Marla says.

"Not typically considered dinner fare," Laurel says.

"It gets worse," Steven says. "The scientist rips off a second leg, yells, 'Jump!' and writes 'five feet' in his notes. After he rips off a third leg and yells, 'Jump!' he writes 'one foot' in his notes. Finally, the scientist rips off the frog's last leg and yells, 'Jump!' The frog doesn't move. 'Jump!' the scientist yells again, but still the frog won't move. For the third time the scientist screams 'Jump!' Still the frog doesn't move." Steven pauses to swallow the last of his iced tea.

"Here comes the punch line," Oscar says. "Take cover."

"So," Steven says, "the scientist writes in his notes,

'After four jumps, frog goes deaf.'"

"Terrible," Laurel says. "Seriously."

"Who's to say what's funny, what's not funny?" Marla says. "Funny's relative."

"No relative of mine," Oscar says.

"Your grandfather was very funny, Oscar," Laurel says.

"You don't get it," Steven says.

"It's not that I don't," Oscar says, sliding a tomato wedge into his mouth. "It's that I do."

"Deaf," Marla says. When she smiles, her teeth line up perfectly, like piano keys. "I just re-told it to myself. It was funnier the second time."

Oscar picks up his bowl, slurps the last of his bisque. Steven crunches croutons, studies the sheen of his son's upper lip. Without the beard, the weakness of the Kliessen chin is exposed. A soft potato.

"Son, how was the bisque?" Steven says. "Easier to eat without a moustache and beard to worry about, yes?"

"Smelled good," Laurel says. "From here."

"When you decided to shave, Oscar, I'm glad you shaved boldly," Steven says. "A goatee isn't a compromise; it's a half-assed beard."

"Where do you stand on muttonchops?" Marla says. "How about the lone moustache?"

"You," Steven says to Marla. "Did you have anything to do with the disappearance of my son's beard?"

"This is the first I've heard of any beard," Marla says. She turns to Oscar and sits back in her chair, pushes herself away from the table for perspective. "It's hard to imagine," she says. She turns back to Steven. "I like yours, though. Distinguished."

"Distinguished," Laurel says. "That's a word people use with beards."

Laurel's the last one finished with her salad, and just as she's pushing it away and wiping her mouth with her napkin, the server arrives with the entrees. Another minute or two between courses might've been appropriate, but Oscar was halfway through his bisque before his mother had swallowed her first bite of lettuce. A group like this is tough to gauge.

"Did I order tuna?" Laurel says.

"You did," Steven says.

"You need your own booth," the server says to Oscar as she sets down his platter of crab legs and his lobster plate. "I could check, see what's available."

"Where he goes, I go," Marla says.

"That's sweet," the server says. "Enjoy."

Oscar's meal came with a bib. Marla stands and circles behind his chair to tie it for him.

"Well, you two," Laurel says. "Your Thanksgiving plans are up in the air, but how about Halloween? Only two weeks away. Any big doings? Dressing up this year? You should team-up. Steven, you and I did that, remember?"

"The cave couple," Steven says.

"Right," Laurel says. "People at the party were saying, 'Oh, you're the Flintstones.' But we weren't the Flintstones. We weren't cartoons. We were live-action cave people. I was adamant, but Steven went with it, yabba-dabba-dooed on command, called me Wilma all night."

"Give the people what they want," Steven says.

"Remember my ballerina year, Steven? It was a few months after I had Oscar. You called my tutu a four-four."

"He didn't," Marla says, seated again and twirling her fork in her shrimp linguini. She uses the bowl of her spoon for leverage. Her first forkful is heavy and tight, no loose ends.

"I don't remember saying that," Steven says, "but I'm sorry."

"There's sorry, and then there's sorry two decades late," Laurel says. "Where was this apology in the 80's? Where was it in the 90's?"

"My werewolf year," Steven says. "I think was my best."

"When were you a werewolf?" Laurel says.

"You don't remember?" Steven says. He takes out his wallet and flips to the picture, slaps it in the center of the table.

"That doesn't look like you, Dad," Oscar says. He's gnawing on the fleshy end of a crab leg like it's a drumstick.

"Halloween, Oscar," Steven says. "The whole idea is not to look like yourself."

"That's not you, Steven," Laurel says. "I don't know who it is, but it's not you. That was the year we hosted the neighborhood party. People used to do that kind of thing," she tells Oscar and Marla.

"If it's not me, then why do I have the picture in my wallet?" Steven says. He's the only one at the table who hasn't yet touched his food. The lemon wedge still rests atop his scallops.

"You didn't dress up that night," Laurel says. "You were irritable for some reason. When people asked, you told them you were disguised as your own twin. Most people didn't laugh."

"Who's the drummer?" Marla says, flipping the werewolf picture and nodding at the snapshot of Oscar.

"Your boyfriend," Steven says.

"No kidding," Marla says. She picks up the wallet and takes a closer look. "I guess you did have a beard." She turns the photo toward Oscar, who looks at it and shakes his head.

"Not me," he says.

"That's you," Steven says. "I snuck a camera into a gig one night. Your Lackawanna gig."

"This guy's playing a set of Ludwigs," Oscar says. "I wish I had Ludwigs. Besides, we never played in Lackawanna."

"I didn't know you drummed," Marla says. "What other secrets are you keeping from me?"

"It's you, Oscar," Steven says.

Oscar takes the wallet from Marla and looks more

closely. "They're not my drums," he says, and flips to the last picture. "Is this Grandpa?"

"Yes," Steven says. "That's Grandpa. He's holding me on his lap. It's my birthday. My first birthday."

"He was handsome," Marla says. "And you were a cutie."

"Let's see," Laurel says, reaching across the table.

Oscar begins to hand the wallet to his mother, but Steven intercepts it. "You're getting it greasy, Oscar," Steven says, refolding the wallet and returning it to his pocket.

"Today's my birthday," Marla says. "I know it's weird announcing it like this, but there you are in the picture, the birthday boy sitting on his father's lap, and today's mine."

Oscar's as surprised as Steven and Laurel. Marla smiles at him and puts her hand over her mouth, like even she's surprised.

"Don't tell me you got the girl nothing," Laurel says.

"It's not his fault," Marla says. "I guess we never got around to exchanging birthdays."

"I feel horrible," Oscar says.

"How were you supposed to know?" Marla says.

"If she didn't tell you," Steven says.

The server swings by to check on them, and Laurel springs into action, pulls the girl's ear down to her mouth, loudly whispers something about birthday cake.

Steven's skeptical, would like a look at Marla's driver's license. What would her motivation be to lie, though? Cake? To be the center of attention? To remind and instruct those around the table that birth is as real and as rampant as death?

"Who's the drummer if not you, Oscar?" Steven says. "Who's the werewolf, Laurel?"

"You're asking questions we don't have answers to," Laurel says.

"Everyone has those, right?" Marla says. "Nagging questions are part of life. I have one. I could just look it up,

I guess, but I never have. I bet none of you knows the answer either. I missed it in a church school version of *Jeopardy!* when I was a kid. My parents were religious for a while. I'm sure the right answer was given, but I forget. This question eliminated me from competition."

"I missed the word 'major' in a spelling bee once," Laurel says. "I thought 'j', but said 'g'. How dumb is that?"

"Here's the question," Marla says. "Actually, no. Forget it."

"Let's hear it," Laurel says.

"I spoke before thinking," Marla says. Her face reddens; her smile fades.

"Go ahead, honey," Oscar says. "It's your birthday."

"Now if I don't say it," Marla says, "the not saying it will be worse, you know?"

"Exactly," Laurel says.

"Well," Marla says. "Here it is. The Bible says that there was one man who never died. When his time came, God just took him up. Who was he?"

"You didn't want to say it because of my father," Steven says.

"I'm sorry," Marla says. "This is insensitive."

"Not at all," Steven says. "We're fine here."

"Jesus," Oscar says.

"No, he died and then lived again," Marla says. "The guy I'm looking for never died in the first place."

Laurel answers "Moses," but Steven knows that's not right. Moses had God for a gravedigger, and that's something, but he still died. Neither Steven nor Oscar can come up with a better answer, though, so conversation moves on.

Steven tells himself he'll look up the answer when he gets home tonight, but with all he has on his mind, chances are he'll forget. If he were to remember, he'd find out that it's not only Laurel's answer that's wrong; it's also Marla's question. There wasn't only one guy; there were a couple. Elijah was one. Instead of breathing a last breath, he caught a ride on a whirlwind, was swept into paradise like a lost kite. Enoch was the other. He just walked off one day. No pomp, no rigmarole. He hiked to heaven, left no trace of himself, no trail-map.

It will be tough for Steven speaking at his father's funeral tomorrow, but even he'd have to admit he's in a better spot than was Enoch's kid, Methuselah. Imagine your father's too good for death, and the eulogy's left to you. At 300, Methuselah hadn't yet reached middle age. His beard was probably still ash black, but long enough that he had to cinch it around his waist like a belt so as not to trip. At Enoch's funeral, though, maybe he let it down. Maybe in lieu of a eulogy, mourners simply formed a line and approached him one by one to dry their tears on his beard, a community face towel. Maybe Methuselah and the other people who'd loved Enoch didn't know what else to do. The world was so young then. Even death wasn't a given. Maybe blubbering one at a time into Methuselah's beard, the ceremony of this, united them in their grief. When Lamech reached the front of the line, wouldn't an embrace have occurred between the tearful son and the damp-bearded father? Wouldn't have Lamech begged Methuselah not to go off on his own anymore in search of Grandpa Enoch? Wouldn't enduring promises have been begged for and made between father and son at that moment?

Had Marla's question been asked and answered correctly, she or Oscar, one of the scientifically-minded, might've proceeded to compare Elijah and Enoch's passages to sublimation, the process by which a solid, like ice, transforms directly into a gas, like vapor. Skips being a liquid altogether. Upon hearing this, Steven's mind might've followed his ears. "Sublimation" to "sublime." He might've thought simply, "To make a funeral beautiful, that would be a good thing." He might've even said this out loud.

Too late now, though. Too far gone. Probably a stretch, anyway.

Laurel's idea about Steven using a few of Charles' jokes tomorrow, though, that might work. There are a few on the fringes of Steven's memory: a charming one about a farmer who takes his pig to a baseball game; a long, convoluted one about a gorilla and a drawbridge; and a racy one about a used car salesman and his promiscuous wife. Tonight, as Steven tosses and turns on the cusp of sleep, maybe he'll call to them, and maybe they'll answer.

Steven watches his table's server and a half-dozen other wait staff approach the table. The cake they haul is small and crooked, but it's ablaze. One of those sparkler candles. The sparks don't last long enough to land on anything. They're here and gone.

The servers horseshoe around the table, turn themselves into a chorus. They look at each other, fill their lungs, and launch into it. The song they sing is not the traditional "Happy Birthday," but something loud and fast. There's clapping, and if you don't clap along, if you don't at least tap your fingers on the edge of the table, you're considered a downer.

Oscar keeps time with his last two crab legs. He's showing off, twirling them in his fingers between taps. Marla's not watching, but the server is. When he tosses one of the legs in the air and catches it, she giggles, bails on the end of the song so that it doesn't end as cleanly as it could've. The hefty server next to her slugs her playfully but solidly in her twig of an arm.

As everyone applauds, Marla leans over Oscar, kisses him wetly in the center of his cheek. More than just a peck, it's a full-fledged smooch. It makes a sound that Steven barely hears, leaves faint lip-marks on Oscar's baby pink jowl that Steven can just barely make out.

LOVE CANAL

Soon after the sins of Hooker Chemical and the city of Niagara Falls were found out, the barrels re-buried, and the homes of Love Canal, depending on proximity to the main dump sites, either bulldozed, boarded up, or fenced off, my family moved to within a few blocks of the neighborhood where babies had been born with withered limbs and extra chromosomes, where the breasts of new mothers had swelled with toxic milk.

My father was thirty-five and just beginning a new career. After more than a decade of working on cars for a living, he decided he'd been called to ministry. When he took the church in Niagara Falls, he'd just graduated from seminary. His Greek and Hebrew were fresh. He said "Shalom" to cashiers and toll booth collectors when they made his change, to waitresses when they warmed his coffee. He owned two suits, one dark and one light, which he wore on alternating Sundays, and when he preached, he wrestled with his glasses, shifting them from pocket to pocket, cleaning them with his handkerchief, sliding them on to read a passage of scripture and then off again to twirl in his fingers as he explained, expounded, and exhorted. If the glasses ended up in his hands at the end of the sermon, when he stretched his arms out over the congregation to deliver the benediction, one of the lenses might catch a spark of sunlight, and I'd imagine the church bursting into flame.

The deacons of the church in Niagara Falls told my father and mother that the parsonage was a few hundred yards too far south to be eligible for automatic buy-out, so they and we were stuck with it. They advised against digging a garden in the backyard, or storing anything of value in the damp basement, but they also offered assurances that tests had been administered, that our new home had been officially declared safe.

My parents accepted this on faith, but on our street there were as many empty houses as neighbors. Occasionally a realtor's "For Sale" sign would appear on the brown lawn of one of these abandoned homes, and my parents would say to each other, "Who do they think they're kidding?" Despite police efforts, drifters, perhaps passing through town on their way to Buffalo or Toronto, squatted in these ghost homes for short stretches to duck the weather or nap, and teenagers occasionally descended on the houses for parties. We'd find fast food bags, cigarette butts, liquor bottles, and condom wrappers in our yard some mornings. One Sunday before leaving for church, I watched from the backseat of the car as my father used a stick to pick up and deposit in our trash can a pair of muddy panties.

The minister my father was replacing in Niagara Falls had left the church and his wife to run off with a married woman from the congregation. Pastor Cox had been counseling the woman and her husband about their deteriorating marriage. In the aftermath of the scandal, many families left the church – some joined other congregations; others stopped attending church altogether – and tithing plummeted. The deacons were up front with my father about these circumstances when they called him to their pulpit. They told him what they needed was a healer, a rebuilder.

Before my father accepted the job, my parents spent a series of evenings in discussion. We lived then in a ground-level one-bedroom apartment in Rochester close to my father's seminary. In winter the snow drifted against our sliding glass patio door, blew away or melted, and then piled up again. It was as if we lived at the bottom half of an hourglass that someone kept flipping.

After my mother bathed my younger sister and put her to bed, my parents would debate the decision freely in front of me, then twelve years old, either because they thought me mature enough to handle or too naïve to understand their disagreement, or because they thought I was sufficiently distracted by the TV or my homework. Besides, there was nowhere else for either of us to go. They couldn't talk in the bedroom they shared with my sleeping sister, the kitchenette offered no privacy, and sending me to bed wasn't an option because the living room couch was where I slept. I loved my sleeping arrangements in that apartment. Many nights I'd watch the muted TV for as long as I could, until every channel had signed off.

One evening as my parents talked, I lay on the wall-to-wall carpet and flipped through a pile of fifty index cards. I had a test coming up, states and their capitals, so on each card I'd written the state on one side and the capital on the other. My father's suggestion. He told me flashcards were how he learned the states and capitals when he was a kid.

My parents didn't raise their voices at each other that night, or ever in that apartment that I can remember – it was too small for yelling just like it was too small for secrets – but I could tell they both were on the verge of getting upset. My mother was speaking more quickly than normal, and my father more slowly. At one point my father snapped his fingers to interrupt my mother, and then I could feel their eyes on me.

"Michigan," my mother said to me quietly.

"Detroit?" I said. "No, wait. Lansing."

"Don't be a guesser," my father said. "Be a knower." And then my mother got up to put the tea kettle on the stove and check on my sister. When she returned a few minutes later, she was balancing two steaming mugs and a glass of milk, and my father and I both rose to help her, and then the two of them, normal-voiced now, resettled into their conversation.

Taking the church in Niagara Falls made my mother uneasy – she told my father that because of all the drama that had taken place, he'd constantly have to be wary of the freshly wounded and the disillusioned – but my father argued that he'd prayed about it, that he believed the Lord was opening a door. He also reasoned that, in one way, it was an ideal situation for a new pastor. He wasn't replacing a beloved retiree, for instance, to whom, in the eyes of some, he'd never measure up. He was replacing an adulterer. "All I have to do to best the last guy is sleep with my wife. A sacrifice I'm willing to make," he said, and in my periphery I watched him slide his arm across the couch cushion toward my mother.

According to what I heard my father tell my mother, according to what the deacons had told him, the latest was that Pastor Cox had decided to leave the ministry altogether. He was biding time as a substitute teacher in Dunkirk where he and the woman were living together in a motel room, paying week-to-week. The woman still had some friends in the church, and she'd told them that she and the pastor were using this time to catch their collective breath, to figure out what should come next. She said they were both sorry and not sorry.

When Pastor Cox left Niagara Falls, his wife had had what I kept hearing referred to as a breakdown. Even by the time my father was hired, this aspect of the situation was still fragile. No one wanted to rush the troubled woman out of the parsonage, but my family needed a place to live.

On the day Mrs. Cox was scheduled to move out of the parsonage and into the apartment the church had arranged for her – we were to move into the parsonage a few weeks later – the U-Haul and crew of volunteers showed up to find her tapping nails into the kitchen wall to hang a new spice rack. She'd just returned from grocery shopping – the kitchen cupboards and refrigerator were freshly stocked – and in the living room, a lush, green jungle of new house plants, still in their black, plastic pots, wound around the edges of the furniture and bloomed on the window sills. The packing boxes which had been dropped off for her a month before were found in the basement, still empty, stacked against one dank wall.

We were still living in Rochester when I heard my mother tell this story to her sister over the phone. It was the weekend before we were to move, and my father was out visiting liquor stores, trying to rustle up boxes. "Our lease is up ten days from today, and there's no Plan B," I heard her say. I think she knew I was listening. I think she felt I had a right to know what she was telling my aunt, but she didn't know if it was right to tell me, or she didn't know the right way to tell me, so she half-told me in this once-removed way.

As we weren't able to move into the parsonage right away, my father, mother, sister, and I were put up in a motel on Niagara Falls Boulevard for three nights. In Niagara Falls, even in winter, all motels are geared for honeymoons. The heart-shaped coffee tables, the complimentary bottles of champagne, the spacious Jacuzzi tubs. At night, the walls are warm to the touch. They vibrate and moan.

My parents re-named our motel the Limbo Inn – they made each other smile saying this – and they tried to keep themselves, my sister, and me busy so the days would pass faster. We spent one afternoon at the Falls. The first time for all of us. Over our heads, in the cold, misty sunlight, gray gulls dodged one another through a field of half-rainbows. On land, everywhere we looked were couples. Even in gloves and mittens they held hands, leaned out in tandem over the railings, blinked down smiling into the static roar of the green and white water.

Twice during my family's first week in the parsonage, Mrs. Cox entered, uninvited, through the front door.

My father wasn't there the first time. He was at church, settling into his new office and working on his first sermon. The TV in the living room was on. My mother watched *General Hospital* when she ironed. As she watched, she tried to keep me from watching. "Not for kids," she'd say if she caught me lingering too long in front of the screen. "Go outside and make some friends."

The sight of Mrs. Cox in our hall startled my mother at first – she put her hand to her throat and dropped one of my father's shirts – but she gathered herself quickly and forced a smile. "Mrs. Cox?" she said. I wondered then and still do now how my mother knew who this woman was. She said the name like a question, but I could tell she wasn't guessing.

Mrs. Cox straightened at my mother's greeting – her puffy eyes widened – but then I watched the truth settle into her thin lips, and her eyes shrunk to slits, and her round shoulders shook as she began to weep. My mother gathered up my sister and set her in her playpen, turned off the TV, and suggested to me that I go upstairs to finish unpacking my bedroom. She then stepped to Mrs. Cox, rested a hand on the woman's narrow back, and asked if she'd like to take off her coat and sit.

I'd already finished setting up my room – I knew my mother knew this – but I understood what she needed from me and didn't argue. Rather than retreat upstairs, though, I disappeared into the kitchen and then down the basement steps with the idea of finding my ice skates which had yet to surface from the move. As I rummaged through the remaining unemptied boxes – the ones my mother had labeled "Misc." with her black marker – I strained to hear the conversation above me, but I couldn't make out words. All I could hear vibrating down through the register were Mrs. Cox's tinny sobs, then my sister's crying, then the whine of the tea kettle, and then the smooth, low hum of my mother's praying voice.

Eventually I heard Mrs. Cox and my mother walk out of the room, the front door open and close, and I watched Mrs. Cox's blurred legs flash by the ice-glazed window above me. I crossed the basement to the other window, the one facing the driveway, and hoisted myself onto the washing machine to watch her walk to her car.

I don't know what made her turn around. I can't remember. I can't figure it out. Perhaps I took myself up on a dare and rapped on the glass; perhaps I accidentally bumped the window while climbing onto the washer. There are other possibilities, of course, that have nothing to do with me. I suppose this woman had many reasons to look back.

When she turned, she looked first to the living room windows. When her eyes finally fell to me, she smiled, glanced once more to the living room, and then walked quickly toward me. I slid off the washer, took a few steps back toward the middle of the basement, and from there watched her drop to the blacktop on her hands and knees, wipe the moisture from the glass with her open palm, and motion to me to come outside. Her loose blouse sagged so I could see her white bra and the tops of her breasts. When I looked at her face, she mouthed words I couldn't make out.

When I heard my mother call my name I was startled. I turned my back to the window and faced the stairs. My heart paused a long time before it beat again. I remember putting my hand on my chest, wondering if I'd be OK, if something dangerous was going on inside me. When I didn't answer my mother, I heard her call again, and when

I didn't answer the second time, I heard the TV come on.

When I finally summoned the courage to turn and look again to the window, Mrs. Cox was gone.

She reappeared a few days later. It was Sunday afternoon. My mother and sister were the guests of honor at a women's welcome luncheon at church, so it was only my father and me at home.

Only a few hours earlier, my father had delivered his first sermon to his new congregation. I'd tried to listen because I sensed what was at stake for him, but I couldn't stop my mind from wandering among the strangers who filled the pews. As I scanned the sanctuary, I tried to see in their faces who they were and what they were beginning to think of my father, if what he was saying was convincing them, and when he prayed, I kept my eyes open and my head unbowed to see how many of them did the same.

My father didn't say her name in his pastoral prayer that morning. I imagine at some point he must've weighed the pros and cons of listing her along with the sick and shut-in he mentioned. Perhaps the choice wasn't entirely his – perhaps the deacons had given him instructions or advice on the matter – but I have to imagine that in the moments following his pulpit prayer, when he invited the congregation to join him in silently presenting their most private and intimate requests to God, that he remembered her then, and that many of those sitting in the pews did too.

Upon entering our home that afternoon, Mrs. Cox called out "Hello" in a jittery but cheerful voice. When my father and I emerged from the kitchen where we'd been eating sandwiches, she smiled through chattering teeth and ran both hands down her body, from the top of her chest to her thighs, as if trying to flatten the wrinkles out of her dress. Her feet and legs were mud-spattered, bare, and sunburn-red, and snowflakes clung to her greasy, feathered hair.

Before my father was able to find his voice to greet her, she made a quick move, caught his face with her hands and tried to pull him toward her. When he pushed her away and turned toward me, I saw a flash of blood on his mouth.

The first time he said my name, I didn't know if he was yelling for help or for me to get away, so I stayed where I was and did nothing. When he was finally able to catch Mrs. Cox's wrists and hold her away from him until she went limp and slumped to the floor, he said my name again, and this time I knew it was for me to get away.

That night, I heard through the wall behind the head-board of my new bed the hushed voices of my parents. At one point I thought I heard my mother sob, but seconds later I heard what sounded like a short burst of muffled laughter from my father. I wished they would stop talking, go to sleep.

When their voices finally quieted, I got out of bed and slipped into the dark hallway. I paused in front of their bedroom door and listened to the silence for a few seconds before easing down the stairs.

I told myself I was going to the living room to watch muted TV like I used to in Rochester, but when I got to the couch, I didn't sit down. I felt my way through the rest of the dark room and into the kitchen until I came to the base-ment door. I opened it, closed it behind me, and without switching on the light, took the steep, narrow steps slowly.

When my bare feet hit the cold floor, I whispered into the dark for her. When I heard her answer – the words she'd mouthed to me through the window, I let myself hear them now – I walked with my hands outstretched until they hit a clammy wall. "You're cold," I said. "Please." Then, my eyes closed to the dark, I leaned for-ward – "Please," I said again. "Please. They're asleep. It's safe" – and I met the cool, musty cement with my lips.

THE DAREDEVIL'S WIFE

Having given his barrel one final once-over – he's checked the seals, greased the hatch hinges, applied a finishing coat of resin to the oak – the daredevil emerges from the basement to attend to his wife. He finds her in the kitchen and interrupts her humming to suggest a penultimate trip to the Falls. Sans barrel, of course. Just the two of them.

Niagara's subdued at night, its roar muffled somehow, its sky empty of daylight's screeching, grimy gulls. The daredevil thinks experiencing the Falls like this could buoy his wife. Steel her for tomorrow. It's her wellbeing the daredevil's considering.

The daredevil's wife takes his invitation wrong, though, hears it as insensitive and irresponsible. She whips her own shoulder with a dishtowel – it sticks, a widow's shawl – and charges the daredevil, burrows her face in his chest, pounds him with soft, half-hearted fists.

She says she's afraid that if she sees the Falls tonight, she'll lose her nerve for tomorrow. Or worse. The daredevil will lose his nerve.

"You're right," the daredevil says. "Of course, you're right."

Otherwise, a calm evening. No eleventh-hour ultimatums, no last-ditch begging. The daredevil and his wife stay home, sip wine, channel-surf.

The daredevil's wife is understandably anxious and distressed, but the daredevil knows, deep-down, she's onboard.

In the beginning the daredevil had difficulty choosing his stunt. Stuck between tightrope and barrel. It was his wife who finally tipped the scales. She said she preferred the barrel's odds, so the daredevil acquiesced. The tightrope would've been problematic anyway. Where and how to string it? What type of knot? Where and how to train? Rope tension? Weather? Wind? How fast is a knot?

The daredevil is not especially handy. His math and science skills are, at best, rudimentary.

With the barrel the daredevil needs only his wife to nudge him into the current and, post-plunge, alert *Maid of the Mist*. No skill is required of him. Science and math be damned. This is the physics of the barrel: curl into a ball and hope. This is the geometry of Niagara: down.

The daredevil's wife asks the daredevil why. Of course she does. Asks him over and over. But the daredevil has no answer. ("The purpose of the plunge is the plunge itself," is what he thinks, but he keeps this to himself, knowing full well it's more non-answer than answer, and he doesn't want to sound flippant. Her question, after all, is legitimate.)

What the daredevil should do is remind himself and his wife of the story of the ark:

"Why?" Noah's wife asks. "God," says Noah. She says, "Seriously." Noah says, "Survival." She says, "Please. Don't be like this." Noah says, "End of the world." She says, "Get over yourself."

Then raindrops, rising water. The ark floats, months pass, the waters recede, the ark runs aground, the dove returns with an olive leaf, the sun re-ignites, and the rainbow appears.

"That's why," Noah says.

The daredevil can't sleep the night before the stunt. Of course he can't. Despite his attempt to be quiet as he climbs out of bed and into his bathrobe and slippers, his wife wakes up. Her head turns on her pillow, and her eyes meet the daredevil's. "Sorry," the daredevil whispers. "Go back to sleep." (When he apologizes again in the morning, she'll tell him she doesn't remember. She'll tell him she has no idea what he's talking about.)

The daredevil takes the basement stairs in the dark. Once his feet hit the cement floor, he shuffles in the direction of the barrel, feeling for it with outstretched arms. When he finds it, he climbs in, closes the hatch, and whispers petitions to his patron saints:

Anna Edson Taylor, who, in taking her plunge, kept a promise made to a classroom of third-graders. The daredevil asks her to guard the integrity of his vessel.

The British barber Charles Stevens, who never resurfaced, leaving behind for rescuers only one tattooed arm. "Guide me with your remaining hand," the daredevil asks. "Deliver me from the undertow."

The obese, would-be poet laureate of the Falls, George Stathakis, who's believed to have died of a heart attack before his barrel even hit the brink, whose blank notebook, fished from the gorge, said more than any sonnet penned in the half-light of the barrel could've begun to say. "Afford me the courage," the daredevil prays, "to transcend even my own descent."

And, finally, Roger Woodward, the barrel-less survivor,

the overboard, seven-year-old, still alive and well saint-by-accident. "Lend me your armor," the daredevil prays. "Your angels."

Just off shore, still barely moving, the daredevil's surprised to hear his wife break into song. He can't quite make out the words, and it's not a tune he recognizes. Something upbeat, though. Sounds like his wife, anyway. Sounds like singing. It's not gulls. Not angels. Not mermaids.

As he drifts into the current, the daredevil wonders: Why sing? To throw off a nosey passerby? To prematurely celebrate the daredevil's success? To keep him company a bit longer? To keep his spirits high? To quell her own fear? The daredevil, again, has no answer.

The barrel caroms off the first rock, rolls over, and begins to pick up speed until it's spinning tight and fast like a centrifuge. The daredevil feels like he's twirling into himself and being pulled apart at the same time. Like he's shrinking, like he's turning inside-out.

As he spins, the daredevil pictures his wife kind of swaying, kind of bopping her head a little as she sings herself back to the parking lot, away from the river and its haze of rainbows.

GREETING PHANTOM

Bradley's freshly-diapered, belly-up on the changing table, gumming one fist. Rachel glides her fingers across her son's ribs, digs lightly in his left pit, plants a raspberry on his ear, but the kid still won't smile. Been stone-faced all day. Rachel's trying not to take it personally.

"You'll be happier after your nap," she says as she gathers him up and settles in the rocker. She has doubts about his sleeping – his eyes are wide open, lidless – but if he doesn't go down for at least an hour this afternoon, tonight will be murder. Best bet's to nurse him, to sweet talk him into it. "You'll eat, then you'll sleep, then you'll smile," Rachel says, her voice soft, sing-songy, like hypnosis.

She lifts her sweatshirt and guides Bradley's head to her breast. He nuzzles, latches on. Rachel puts her pinkie in the palm of his hand, feels him squeeze, release, squeeze, almost in rhythm. It's a fact Bradley likes his hands busy. Grown, he'll be like his father: a thumb-twiddler, a knuckle-cracker. A guy constantly in his own hip pocket, fiddling with keys and loose change.

There's only minor fussing when they switch breasts, and to Rachel's surprise, Bradley's down and out in his crib within twenty minutes. Rachel covers him with a blanket, runs the tip of her finger around the curve of his ear. When Bradley sleeps, his lids flutter open. You can see half of each eyeball. Weird, but more cute than creepy, like he might be possessed by an other-worldly presence, but adorably so. Bradley's grandma says Rachel used to fall asleep open-eyed, too. So it's genes. Bradley also has Rachel's long neck and her widow's peak. Quinn traits in Bradley? Other than busy hands, jury's still out. Rachel's sure they're there. A kid has layers, like an archeological dig. Bradley's first joke, first temper tantrum, first crush: each will be an unearthing of sorts. Rachel could keep a tally sheet on the refrigerator. A Quinn column, a Rachel column. Of course it's not that tidy. There has to be a third column under a question mark or an ampersand or maybe the infinity symbol, those two side-by-side ovals. Bradley's more than the sum of his parts. This is his salvation. This is everyone's.

As Rachel closes Bradley's bedroom door behind her, she hears a car pull into the apartment building's lot. If it's Quinn, he's home early. Rachel hopes this doesn't mean a premature end to Bradley's nap. Once the boy's down he's generally a good sleeper, but Quinn's noises wake him. When Rachel's allergies kick in, she'll string together window-rattling sneezes like words in a sentence, and Bradley won't stir, but if Quinn clears his throat two rooms away, the kid's up and at 'em. One afternoon last week, Rachel risked hanging a picture during nap time. She hammered a nail into the wall just outside Bradley's door, and the boy slept right through. Minutes later, though, Quinn came home, clanked together some hangers in the closet as he hung up his jacket, and Bradley erupted.

Rachel clips the nursery monitor to her jeans on her way to the living room. If it was Quinn's car she heard, she hopes he'll at least make an effort to keep it down. Entering the apartment via the hall door rather than coming in off the patio would be a good start. The sliding glass door is off its runner – Rachel never uses it because she can't budge it – but Quinn isn't deterred. He wrestles it open, wrestles it closed. Calls it his afternoon workout. Metal grating on metal, fingernails on a chalkboard. And then there's his mouth. He has one of those voices that carries. Worst case scenario is he'll come in singing – whatever song he last heard on his car radio; he seems to know them all – then go through the idiotic production of greeting Phantom. Quinn's taken to blaming Phantom for Bradley's ruined naps like Rachel's Uncle Reid used to blame his macaw for passing gas.

At the patio window, Rachel sees Terrence, the kid from upstairs, approaching the building. It must've been his car she heard. Rachel's surprised twice: first, that Terrence's car is running; second, that he's wearing his Subway uniform. He'd recently told Quinn he was going to quit. "Six-inch or twelve-inch," he'd said. "In my sleep."

It's no time at all before Rachel hears Terrence's TV come on. One of the music channels. It will be on when Rachel and Quinn turn in tonight, and it will be on in the morning when Bradley wakes them. Not too loud, nothing to justify a complaint, but the constant overhead drone wears on Rachel. She'd almost have Terrence turn it up so she could hear more clearly what it is that's disturbing her.

It's been nearly a month now of the all-night TV, nearly a month since Terrence's girlfriend, Kiki, and their baby have been gone. Could be just a long vacation, an extended visit with family. That's the hope, but Rachel suspects something sadder, suspects strongly enough that she's reluctant to come right out and ask. Quinn says she shouldn't stick her nose in or jump to conclusions – Rachel finds his reluctance to join in the speculation half admirable, half frustrating – but she can't help imagining sad scenarios. In some Terrence comes off as the heavy; others vilify Kiki.

Rachel walks over to the coffee table, re-assembles the stray sections of the newspaper, and collapses on the couch. When she leans her head back and shuts her eyes, Terrence's TV goes to commercial. The volume goes up slightly, and Rachel thinks she hears the phrase "Not available in stores."

The truth of the matter is, Terrence seems like a good kid – Kiki does, too – and Rachel and Quinn feel invested. They're the ones who told the younger couple about the apartment upstairs when it came open, and Quinn's dropped off Terrence at Subway a few times when the kid's car wouldn't start. The babies, Bradley and Daphne, are the same age, born within a couple weeks of each other. That's how the couples met, at the pre-natal and birthing classes at the hospital. Terrence and Kiki were obviously the youngest parents-to-be there. Rachel guessed they were around seventeen or eighteen, almost a whole decade younger than her and Quinn and most of the others. Terrence didn't look up once during the first night's introductions. He had his baseball cap pulled down so low Rachel couldn't be sure he had eyes or a nose.

The nervousness, embarrassment, and fear Rachel had sensed in Terrence set him apart from the other men attending the classes, Quinn included. From them, Rachel caught a whiff of self-congratulation. The fact they were there at all showed them to be sensitive and responsible, and the swollen women sitting next to them served as evidence of their virility. Double-ply self-satisfaction. When a woman attended alone, she'd come equipped with an excuse for her partner: he was helping waterproof a buddy's basement, picking up some overtime hours, or attending to the needs of his children from a prior relationship. When Quinn would talk about the absentee men in the car on the way home, he'd tell Rachel how lucky she was to have him. He was trying to be funny, ironic – it was supposed to come across that he didn't actually believe she was at all lucky being stuck with him – but behind the joke, Rachel detected genuine pride. She still detects it now and then.

When Rachel discovered she was pregnant with Bradley, she and Quinn weren't a couple. Despite this, he'd left Cleveland to be with her in Albany when he got the news. His own initiative. Rachel hadn't asked or expected-initially, she wasn't even sure she wanted him to come-but now that he's here, she's trying to see the potential, trying to give it every chance, for Bradley's sake if for no other reason, and she's been heartened by the bond she's seen form between father and son. Not even a half-year in the world, and Bradley's smitten. Quinn walked into the living room with his toothbrush in his mouth this morning, and Bradley's cheeks bunched into a grin. The inherent humor in oral hygiene. Quinn leaned down, touched the tip of his son's nose with the sudsy bristles, and the boy was electrified with delight. His hands opened and closed beside his ears like he was trying to snatch out of the air the jabber-jabber words his father cooed at him.

"Real words, Quinn," Rachel had said. "His development."

"Words are cheap," Quinn answered. "Me and my boy, we understand each other."

Rachel lifts her legs onto the couch and pulls an afghan over them. She knows she shouldn't fall asleep, but she's tired. Bradley tires her; Quinn tires her. Two kinds of tired. Tired doesn't mean things aren't good, though; tired doesn't mean there aren't things to feel good about. Maybe things are even better than Rachel would've predicted had she allowed herself to make a prediction. She knows, though, that what matters finally is how things end up. It's still early. The milestones of this family are still measured in months. She and Quinn have been together for eight, Quinn's been full-time at Troybilt for seven, and Bradley's been in the world for five.

Former high school sweethearts meet by chance one afternoon at a grocery store salad bar in Cleveland. His apartment's a block away; they can catch up there. A few weeks later, back in Albany, back in real life, she discovers they've made a baby, and against all odds and good sense, the sweethearts re-unite to make a go of it.

It could be a movie. But what's that mean? Movies can rip you up. They can send you squinting into the brightly lit lobby dazed and weeping. Quinn's a hero because he hopped on I-90? Traveled from Ohio to New York? A fish can do that. A trash fish, a bottom-feeder. Wiggle your fins long enough along the bottom of Lake Erie and you'll cross state lines. The question's no longer about arriving, it's about staying. Quinn's a hero because he gave up a low-paying warehouse job in Cuyahoga Falls for a low-paying factory job in Troy? Because he went from stacking boxes to assembling rototillers? Is that a sacrifice or, at worst, a parallel move?

In Rachel's case, there's no question what she gave up. She was on the move at the bank. When Vicki switched branches to shorten her commute, who but Rachel would've gotten the head teller promotion? Vicki had told Rachel as much at the baby shower. Vicki said she respected Rachel's decision to keep the baby, admired her desire to stay home for a few years to devote herself full-time to motherhood, but behind Vicki's words, Rachel thought she detected some disappointment, even disapproval. So who's the greater sacrificer? Is there even any contest?

Rachel knows the danger inherent in this line of thinking, where it can lead. She knows a relationship shouldn't become a competition. She's seen the shows, read the articles. She knows she shouldn't keep score. She knows if this is going to work, she and Quinn have to be on the same team, have to communicate. This is the trick. Signals are sent from one partner to the other only to be missed or misinterpreted, especially early on. So Rachel's trying not to read too much into anything, but, on the other hand, she doesn't want to make the mistake of not reading enough into something. Quinn's car, for example. Rachel would have him ditch his Ohio plates for New York plates. She'd at least like him to get a New York driver's license. Make something official. All you have to do is wait in line. There will be harder assignments than this. There already have been. What's more, Rachel knows there are still boxes in Quinn's trunk from his move. Full boxes. There's plenty of room in the apartment. When she tells him to unpack and stay a while, though, he says he'll get to them eventually, that he's not even sure what's in them. But that's not the point, Rachel wants to tell him. If you're in two places at once, you're nowhere.

"What do you have in that trunk? Old girlfriend memorabilia?" Rachel asked him about a month ago. She worked to keep a smile on her face. "Souvenirs from your single days? Little black books and bottles of cologne? Back issues of *Hustler*?"

Quinn mirrored Rachel's smile. "That man is no more," he said. "Not a trace of him left. Nothing but a ghost."

"Spooky story," Rachel said. "Is it true?"

"Boo," Quinn said. "Boo hoo."

It wasn't long after that Quinn dreamed up Phantom, brought him home. "He can be rambunctious," Quinn explained that first day. "Phantom's full of energy."

"Somebody's full of something," Rachel had said. She knew Quinn liked games, liked to tease, but this gag seemed more off-the-wall than usual, and she wasn't sure how to respond. She'd been folding laundry on the couch and was flanked by stacks of underwear and socks. No room for Quinn. Bradley sat in his swing not swinging, sucking his pacifier. His own hands mesmerized him. His fingers danced in front of his face like sign language.

"Phantom will settle down when he settles in," Quinn said as he stretched out on the floor between Rachel and Bradley. "Key is to stay on top of him, balance firmness with understanding. And no days off."

"Is this for Bradley's benefit?" Rachel said. "Is this some sort of imagination exercise the whole family can play? Is this *Romper Room*? Some sort of riddle? Am I supposed to guess? Is Phantom a pet? An orphan? A long lost relative? An old drinking buddy? Your imaginary friend from childhood all grown up?"

Quinn rose to his knees and crawled to Bradley. When he took the pacifier out of his son's mouth, Bradley beamed, gurgled. "Phantom's Phantom," Quinn said.

"I'm really not in the mood," Rachel said. "Not even close. My boobs hurt. I was overcome this morning reminiscing about caffeine."

"I'm here for you," Quinn said. "I'm there for you."

"This Phantom thing is you trying to tell me something?" Rachel said. "You feel invisible because all my attention goes to Bradley? Is this sulking? Is this half joke, half you making a point? Am I in an argument I didn't know about?" Rachel pulled a sock from the laundry basket and slipped it over her hand. "Hi, Quinn," the sock said in a high-pitched voice. "I'm Rachel's imaginary messenger. Word is she'll be able to devote herself to showering you with affection on a full-time basis as soon as Bradley graduates high school."

Quinn returned the pacifier to Bradley's mouth and turned his head to address the empty space to his left. "You learn not to take it personally, Phantom. Breastfeeding, post-partum, the moon. It's difficult telling what's genuine meanness, what's hormones."

Rachel balled the sock and bounced it off Quinn's ear. Bradley spit out his pacifier to giggle.

Three weeks later, Phantom's still a presence. This past weekend, Rachel, deciding she'd had enough, tried to exorcise Phantom while Quinn was at work. If Quinn was just picking on her, trying to get a rise out of her simply because that's what people who live together do, that was one thing, but she sensed Quinn's schtick was taking a different, darker turn. Hearing him blame Phantom for an empty milk carton in the refrigerator or a raised toilet seat was one thing, but seeing Phantom's signature underneath

Quinn's on her birthday card was something else entirely. So she'd come up with a plan to get across to Quinn the message that enough was enough, that he needed to stop while he was ahead, but she also wanted to demonstrate that she had it in her to be a good sport, that she could dish as well as take.

She'd thought her story was good. The ski-masked perps were two well-built males – breathtakingly well-built, she'd told Quinn – but she hadn't gotten the plate number of their black van, and although she remembered the sunlight glinting off something metallic, she couldn't say for sure whether it was a knife, a gun, or a foil-wrapped sandwich. At any rate, she said, she'd sensed in Phantom's demeanor an air of resignation. He hadn't resisted. It was as if he'd been expecting them, as if he were relieved they'd finally showed. Rachel had seen everything through Bradley's bedroom window. She'd tried to discourage the abductors by rapping lightly on the glass and making a stern face. She wishes she could've done more, but she didn't want to ruin Bradley's nap. "I know in my head it wasn't my fault," Rachel told Quinn, "but that doesn't ease the guilt in my heart." When Quinn didn't respond – he'd obviously been caught off-guard – Rachel added, "Please understand this is something I'm going to have to live with."

Phantom was gone seventy-two hours, but on Wednesday evening, upon returning home from the grocery store, Rachel found Quinn, Bradley, and Phantom playing on the living room carpet. "Miracle!" Quinn said. "You should've seen Bradley's face!"

Who could know the tragedy Phantom had escaped or what anguish he'd endured? What mattered, of course, was that he was home. Quinn said Phantom didn't appear to have been physically harmed but suggested it was difficult to know just by looking what psychological damage had been done. He asked Rachel to join him in showing Phantom some extra attention for a while. "He needs to feel secure," Quinn said. "You need to help me love him up."

When the monitor on her hip erupts with a cough, Rachel rubs her eyes, stands, holds her breath, and braces for the scream. When it doesn't come, she's relieved. Once the boy wakes up, there's no restarting the nap, no second chances.

The humming TV voices above her head give way to a muffled drumbeat. Rachel stares at the ceiling, wonders where blame should be assigned. Terrence? The building's architect? Herself? Quinn's not bothered by Terrence's TV. Rachel will say, "You don't hear that?" and he'll say, "Hear what?"

Rachel sits back down, picks up the remote, switches on her own TV, and starts flipping. There are five music channels on top of each other: CMT, VH1, BET, MTV, MTV2. When Rachel hits MTV2, she turns up the volume. Tit for tat. Fire with fire. If you can't beat 'em. As long as Bradley doesn't wake up.

The video's one of those female pop singer, male rapper duets. The rapper has the pop singer backed against a bucking SUV. He looks at her chest as he raps his proposition. Then the pop singer turns the tables, backs the rapper against the SUV and waves her long finger in his face as she sings her answer that says one thing, means another.

As Rachel watches the performers grind on each other, she hears their give-and-take being turned up overhead. Can Terrence hear her TV? It could be he's turning up the volume as a friendly gesture – he wants Rachel to know he too likes the song – or it could be defiance, like he wants her to know he'll play his TV as loudly as he wants.

Rachel's not sure she has Terrence's phone number, but she has two feet, doesn't she? To sit and stew about the TV is pointless. Same goes for wondering about Kiki and Daphne. Neighbors should talk. It's one flight of stairs for hell's sake. She can take the monitor with her, and Bradley's breathing is deep and steady. Rachel turns off the TV and slips on her sneakers. She pushes the button on the knob, locking the door behind her, and heads to the stairwell.

Standing in front of Terrence's door at the top of the stairs, Rachel considers backing down, wonders if she's about to push someone who shouldn't, at present, be pushed. Before she can retreat, though, the door opens, and Terrence is standing in front of her, tapping his bare chest with his remote. This is the first time Rachel's seen him without a hat, without a shirt.

"Rachel," he says. "I thought I heard someone. What's up?"

"Hey, Terrence," Rachel says. "Been a while." She hadn't before realized how skinny Terrence is. He wears his clothes so baggy, it's difficult to tell much about the body underneath. His chest is narrow, his shoulders pointy.

"You want to come in?" Terrence says, moving aside, opening the door wider. "You want a Coke? I got Cokes."

Terrence smells like cold meat and cut onions, and his eyes are pink and puffy. Rachel senses he's not just being polite. He sincerely wants her to come in to drink one of his Cokes.

"Sure." Rachel steps inside and closes the door behind her. Terrence has already switched off the TV and is on his way to the kitchen.

"Glass or out of the can?" Terrence says.

"Don't dirty a glass," Rachel says. She moves into the middle of the apartment. The couch is set between two molded-plastic patio chairs, and the TV, a huge flat-screen, is centered against the back wall. In one corner of the living room is a baby swing, and a folded high-chair leans against the wall, separating the living room from the kitchen. The carpet is spotless. This surprises Rachel. She's never heard a vacuum.

Terrence emerges from the kitchen with two glasses and hands Rachel one. The ice cubes crackle.

"Thanks," Rachel says.

"Sit," Terrence says, sinking into the couch. "My TV get you up here? Too loud?"

"Just checking in," Rachel says, settling on the other end of the couch. "Haven't run into you guys in a while."

Terrence nods his head. "How's Bradley? And Quinn?" He smiles. "Both your boys."

"One's working and one's sleeping," Rachel says. She pats her monitor. "I need two of these, right? Or maybe I've got the wrong one wired."

Terrence smiles again. "What some couples do," he says. "Cell phones, beepers, two-ways. Keep tabs 24-7. No wiggle room."

Rachel looks down to the glass of Coke in her lap. "How about Daphne and Kiki? Your two girls?"

"Still no change," Terrence says. He leans forward to balance his glass on the carpet and then leans back, locks his hands behind his neck. "Like I've been telling Quinn."

"Quinn?" Rachel says. "Did he come in for a sub today?"

"No, haven't seen him today, but, you know, he pokes his head in up here every once in a while," Terrence says. "Anyways, what was wrong with Daphne when they admitted her is still wrong. 'No news isn't good news, but it's not bad news, either.' That's what one doctor told Kiki this week. Think about it, though. That means nothing. They know nothing. That's what the doctor was saying, or getting around saying. I don't tell this to Kiki, of course. She's there bedside. She doesn't need to be hearing that from me."

Rachel feels like she's been hollowed, like the inside of her body is the inside of a balloon. Through the monitor Bradley sighs loudly as if he's deeply disappointed or satisfied.

"Baby boy's having himself a dream," Terrence says. "What's the range on those things? How far before he fades?"

"What is it exactly?" Rachel says. "With Daphne. What's the matter?"

"Like I said, they still don't know," Terrence says. He hunches forward, rests his elbows on his knees. "She still can't keep anything down. They're still feeding her through a tube."

"She's at Albany Medical?"

"Albany Medical? If she were there, don't you think I'd be there?" Terrence doesn't use his arms to push himself off the couch, he jumps up, barely missing his drink with his foot. He begins to walk in the direction of the kitchen but stops and turns before he gets there.

"I'm sorry," Rachel says. "You don't need me upsetting you."

"No," Terrence says. "I'm sorry. I'm embarrassed now. I guess I thought you'd know. That you knew. Baltimore. That's where they've got Daphne."

"Johns Hopkins? That's a great hospital, Terrence. That's something to feel positive about."

"That's where the specialists are. But I'm confused about that because no one knows what's wrong. These specialists who are supposed to help Daphne, they specialize in what exactly? Unknown diseases? How can you specialize in something unknown?"

"Maybe they specialize in diagnosing," Rachel says. "They figure out what's wrong, and then another team takes over. The curing specialists."

"That's pretty much what Quinn said, too," Terrence says. He sits down again next to Rachel and eases his head back against the top of the couch. His bare ribs jut out like gills. Rachel remembers thinking this about Bradley's ribs when he was a newborn. She'd wondered if her boy was short on skin.

When the monitor crackles, Rachel stands. She hears Bradley's bedroom door open.

"Old man's home," Terrence says.

He's a good looking boy, isn't he? The voice in the monitor is a heavy whisper. The speaker's talking directly into the receiver. *Takes after his mother. Where do you suppose she is? Gone for good? You think she's had enough? You think she's listening? Hey, Bradley's mom, you got your ears on?*

"Kiki should be calling," says Terrence. "This is usually about the time. After my shift."

Don't worry. She's probably just down the hall in the laundry room. If she has split, though, it's up to you and me to raise this kid.

Rachel switches off the monitor. "I should get back."

"Who's Quinn talking to?" Terrence says, standing to walk Rachel to the door. "That is Quinn, right? You guys have company?"

Rachel puts her hand on Terrence's bony shoulder and squeezes. He feels cold. She wants to tell him to take a hot shower, to put a shirt on. "I'll have a good thought for Daphne," she says. "Tell Kiki I said so."

"I'll keep the TV down," Terrence says. "You won't even know I'm up here."

"Please," Rachel says as she steps into the hall, "I don't want that," and she tries to smile – she thinks he sees it – before the door closes. Just as it latches, she hears his phone ring. It rings five times before he picks up.

Rachel takes the stairs halfway down and then has to stop to sit. She remembers this feeling from pregnancy. Your body shuts down without asking first, without getting permission. You get tired from the inside out.

When she switches the monitor back on, she hears that Bradley's awake. He's shrieking and giggling. *Bzzz,* the voice says. Rachel knows this game. Your finger's the bee. It starts high above your head, twirling in a lazy, innocent circle, and then takes a sudden dive into Bradley's belly button. It's sure-fire. You can see the anticipation in the boy's eyes. He can't wait to be stung. She should've thought of it before.

What Quinn's kept from her isn't even a secret. At the moment, Rachel can't imagine knowing someone less. That's partly the reason for the tears she's fighting.

Of course, there's also sympathy for Daphne, and there's guilt, too. Bradley's well. It's almost satisfying to imagine Bradley so sick because she gets to snap out of it and remember what's true. Rachel wonders if Quinn's mind worked this way when he first heard about Daphne, wonders how else it might've worked.

I'll take care of discipline, you handle nurturing. Good cop, bad cop. We'll switch roles at puberty to keep him on his toes.

If Rachel had the key, if she had a crowbar, she'd head to the parking lot and pop Quinn's trunk. She'd bring in the boxes herself or maybe march them to the dumpster. Maybe forget the trunk altogether and take a whack or two at the windshield.

Rachel stands and catches her breath, descends the rest of the stairs. At the door to the apartment, she grabs the knob. Locked. She realizes she forgot to take her key with her. Quinn must've used the patio door.

Remember watching her clip coupons in the morning? Before living here, I didn't know people still did that. Now, though, nothing says home to me like the whisper of scissors at the breakfast table. She'll be missed.

Rachel balls her hand, raps with her knuckles. When the door doesn't open, she bangs with the side of her fist, her forearm. If she had a crowbar. She lands a couple kicks. Like she's locked in rather than out. The monitor on her belt repeats each blow.

THE WRONG HANDS

Before I started working out at Titan's Gym seven months ago, before I met Teddy, I was a mess. On my way out. I'm not exaggerating. Facts are facts. Lives like the one I was living don't tend to last.

It was New Year's Day that I clipped the coupon for a free one-week membership. I spotted it on the last page of the Sports section, next to an ad for an escort service, and I couldn't ignore it. Despite the haze of my hangover, I saw my situation clearly that morning. Sitting there at my kitchen table, a freshly opened hair-of-the-dog beer in front me, I asked myself point-blank, "Do you want to live or die?" and when I couldn't answer myself straight, when I heard myself hem and haw, when I looked up from the paper and out the window just in time to catch a glimpse of my neighbor's bag-of-bones black cat streaking across my frozen front yard with some bloody, broken creature jammed in its mouth, I knew the nature of my crisis.

During that first month of workouts, instead of feeling better, I felt worse, like I was rushing my own ending. I felt deathbed bad. Pistol-whipped-and-left-in-an-alley bad.

I got sick in the locker room after every workout. Worse than having my face in a public toilet, though, was putting up with the group of eavesdropping muscleheads standing outside the stall, thumbs in their weight belts, taking glee in my plight. This wasn't humor for thinkers. That said, on more than one occasion my grunting and hacking had the whole locker room in stitches.

My first vomit-free workout was Groundhog's Day. I almost lost it in the parking lot – I coughed and gagged, turned some heads – but finally was able to keep myself together. When I walked into the locker room the next day, everyone's clapping my back, calling me buddy, calling me guy, calling me pal, telling me to have a good workout. Like I'd passed some kind of initiation. Charity, the girl working the desk, actually takes the cell phone out of her ear to say goodbye to me when I sign out. Calls me by my name. "Goodbye, Elliot." Like we're chums. Like I'm worthwhile. Like I exist. This is notable because just a week before, while signing in, I told her I liked how her tangerine jogging suit matched her tangerine sports drink, and the look she gave told me to keep walking, told me it wasn't as much what I'd said as it was that I'd said anything at all.

Teddy McGuiness, one of the chief muscleheads, is a bonafide friend of mine now. I didn't know him well those first couple months at Titan's, but once in a while, when none of his buddies was within earshot, he'd offer an encouraging word, tell me to keep the faith. "Soon the endorphins will kick in, and it'll be smooth sailing." I'd nod at his broad back as he walked away, but I wasn't totally buying it. I know now, though, he was right. I've become a believer. The word "endorphins" reminds me of the word "dolphins," and that's how I imagine them. Tiny dolphins swimming around in my bloodstream, torpedoing themselves up to break the surface, leaping and turning, unfolding gracefully into perfect dives, then slipping back cleanly into the drink. Scenes like this pop into my head during workouts, especially while I'm doing cardio. Since summer arrived, Teddy and I skip the treadmills and elliptical trainers and head outside to run. Titan's isn't far from the Lake, just a few blocks, so after lifting we run this three-mile loop that takes us down to the water, to Dobbins Landing and the Bicentennial Tower, along a stretch of the bike trail that follows the shoreline, and then back up the hill, back to the gym. On Saturdays, when we have more time, we sometimes drive over to Presque Isle to run on the beach.

You tell people you live in Erie, Pennsylvania, and unless they're fishermen, they moan for you or tilt their heads sympathetically or make some comment about The Mistake by the Lake, which — they don't have their facts straight — is actually Cleveland, or about lake effect snow, which, it's true, buries us five, even six months out of the year, but you know you could change their minds by showing them the Peninsula in summer. At any rate, running in sand makes for a great workout, and it's easy on the ankles and shins. Time passes faster, too. You forget to check your watch sometimes and end up running longer than you'd planned. Even though Teddy and I sometimes talk while we run, it happens a lot that I'll start watching the water — maybe I'll see a gull dive or a fish jump — and my mind will make that leap to dolphins, to endorphins, and then I'll start feeling them, little pulses and ripples in my chest, hamstrings, and glutes. Even in my groin.

Teddy does cardio because he knows he has to, not because he likes to. He's not a natural runner. He'd much rather pump iron. The guy's huge. When we're running on the beach, you should see the heads turn. At the club, too. His pecs enter a room a good full second before the rest of him. His shoulders, his lats, his delts. He has to angle himself down hallways. The drinking fountain just outside the weight room is set back in this narrow enclave, essentially off-limits to Teddy because he can't fit, so I take his bottle and fill it for him when I fill mine. Otherwise, he'd have to hike back to the locker room or buy designer water out of the vending machine at a buck-fifty a pop. All that Teddy's done for me, I'm more than glad to help out.

Teddy's only in his late-twenties – I have almost a full decade on him – but I can't help seeing him as a kind of role model. Not just in terms of fitness. He's got something else I've never had but always wanted, and I think hanging around him is helping me understand how to get it. It's hard to explain what this "it" is. I know it when I see it in Teddy, though, and know it when I don't see it in myself.

When he spots for me on bench for instance. I'll be on my last rep, seeing nothing but gold and red flashes and feeling nothing but fire as I try to push it out, and Teddy won't lift a finger until I'm stuck and losing ground. "Up to the sky, Elliott! Up to the sky! From your chest! Breathe!" he yells at me, but flat on my back and straining, I feel like I can't breathe, and my arms start to fail, and the bar starts to sink, and spit's flying out the sides of my mouth, and my nose is running, and I want to surrender. I want to live to fight another day. I'm empty. Nothing left. At this moment, Teddy reaches under the bar and steadies it, stops it from falling, but he doesn't let me quit. "Come on, pussy," he growls. "Work it out. Show me something," and he won't budge that bar until he feels me pushing on it.

The first few times I got stuck like that on the bench, I afterwards felt angry, like I'd been bullied and needed to stand up for myself. I was too spent to act, though, and I'm glad because I now understand what Teddy's up to, what he's after. My own good. We're a team now, even though sometimes in the middle of things it might not feel like this.

Teddy floats around the area schools as a substitute gym teacher these days, but he's considering a career change, thinking toward becoming a personal trainer. He sees me as a project, I think. A guinea pig. At any rate, I'm more than willing, feel lucky things have turned out like they have with him and me. It wasn't long after getting to know each other that Teddy had me on his schedule. Mondays,

Wednesdays, and Fridays are chest, arms, and abs; Tuesdays, Thursdays, and Saturdays are back and legs. Each of these days, on top of the lifting, we do forty-five minutes of cardio. And he's got me eating right. Simple carbs, fatty meats, and dairy are out. Caffeine, too. I'll stop for a drive-thru cappuccino once in a while, but I rarely get the whole cup down before guilt consumes me and I feel led to dump the rest out my window. Water, decaf green tea, and nonfat soymilk are my beverage options.

I'm a machine is what Teddy's taught me. Garbage in, garbage out. You can't pollute the endorphins' habitat. Brown rice, soy cheese, and boiled eggs taste better if you think about your body when you eat them. Beer, potato chips, and ice cream taste worse. I'm not saying it isn't hard sometimes – you should've seen how I ate prior to meeting Teddy, and it's true that the worst habits are the hardest to break – but it's getting easier.

To help me stay on the straight and narrow, Teddy makes me a copy of his weekly menu. This is a big help. Say I come home from the gym one evening with pizza on my mind. Maybe some of the other guys on my shift ordered one in for lunch – I've been punching the clock over at GE since I graduated high school – or I heard a Papa John's or Pizza Hut ad on the radio that I can't get out of my mind, or I found coupons in my mailbox. It's amazing, the power of suggestion. Anyway, part of the reason I'm able to resist is because I know Teddy is across town in his kitchen preparing exactly what I should be preparing in mine. What I'm saying is we're there for each other even when we're not actually there.

Like Teddy, I live alone, so this helps cut down on temptation. I don't have to watch someone across the table from me gorging on fettuccini Alfredo as I'm eating my baby spinach and tuna, but on occasion when I eat dinner at a restaurant or get together with extended family on holidays, what I feel toward the other diners isn't jealousy. It's pity. It's like I have x-ray vision and can see their arteries clogging, their hearts straining, their poor endorphins floating on the surface, belly up, fins limp, little lifeless x's where their eyes should be.

Sundays, Teddy and I make ourselves stay away from Titan's even though it's where we want to be. Muscles need recovery time. This summer we've been spending our off-day together. It's the next best thing to being at the gym. I have a grill, and I have cable, and I have air conditioning, so we meet at my house. The neighbor's cat, that same hunter who crossed my front lawn New Year's Day with his jaws full of fresh game, appears as soon as I fire up the grill, like he's been waiting all week for us to get the show on the road, and Teddy and I toss him chunks of the salmon or chicken breast we're eating before we head inside to watch a ballgame, go over the menu for the week, and once in a while even split a light beer if Teddy's feeling like we've been exceptionally good. Light beer is bad beer – let's face it – but on these Sundays it tastes almost OK.

When I pull into Titan's parking lot, even if there are closer spaces available, I instinctively head back to the northeast corner to find a spot. I don't know why, but we muscleheads gravitate there, just like all the Pilates ladies gravitate up front near the doors, like all the racquetball players gravitate to the side lot by the dumpster. No one decreed this segregation; it just happened.

So I know the rides of most of the regular weightlifters. Phil's F-150, Keenan's cold weather Subaru and his warm weather Harley, and the guy Keenan's always with, the guy who wears the headband, his Olds. Teddy drives this tiny Honda. He says getting in and out of it helps keep him flexible. And Preacher's Astro Van. Preacher and his wife have kids out the wazoo. I peeked in the window of the van once and counted four booster seats.

Preacher is called Preacher at the club not because he's a minister but because he does set after set of preacher curls.

He can't get enough of them. Teddy and I don't do them.
They look painful as hell. When I watch Preacher do
them, I can't help but cringe. You rest your arms on this
podium-like a preacher delivering a sermon, I guess? – but
the podium slopes away from you instead of toward you.
The idea is that your arms can't swing – you can't cheat –
so you're able to zero in on your biceps, forearms, and
wrists. Preacher's not that big of a guy – even I've got
broader shoulders, a more developed chest – but he's got
these Popeye arms exploding out of his shirt sleeves.
Because he doesn't do enough core work, though, his arms
look like they don't belong to him. Like he's borrowing
them from someone else. An NFL lineman maybe, or one
of those WWF monsters. Teddy asks him, "You got a per-
mit for those guns, Preacher?" and it makes everyone in
the weight room who hears it, Preacher included, happy.

I understand what Preacher was thinking in wanting to
tag along with Teddy and me. I'm not cold-hearted. I'm
not mean. I'm not incapable of sympathy. I was fine with
Preacher shooting the bull with us in the locker room and
the sauna, was even fine with him starting to work in with
us on bench. I admit to feeling put upon, though, when he
showed up unannounced at my house one Sunday, evidently inviting himself to lunch. He comes bearing a half-
dozen beef patties, but they're not ground sirloin, they're
ground chuck – like Teddy and I would ever eat that
garbage – and along with the burgers, he's toting a case of
Railbender Ale, a local brew that, previously, was one of
my favorites. Now, of course, though, it's a problem.
Again, it's not that I don't get where the guy's coming
from. His house is swamped with kids, and his wife isn't
much of a fan of his anymore – these are his words – so I
understand his desire to get in on the good thing Teddy
and I have going, and maybe, theoretically, a third wheel
would be all right if it were the right third wheel, but
Preacher's not the right third wheel. He's a guy who talks
too much, a conversation bully. He says some compelling

things now and then – the guy's obviously bright; his inter-
ests are broad – but you're exhausted after listening to
him. Every exchange is a wrestling match.

Despite it being my endorphins' day of rest, as
Preacher sinks into my couch and starts talking, they com-
mence popping and flipping like I'm running uphill.
Teddy and I are trying to hear the ball game we have on,
but Preacher's revved. He's using up all the air in the
room. It takes him two full innings to explain the dynam-
ics of static electricity after we see this commercial for a
no-batteries flashlight. When you need it, you just shake it
and switch it on. The Excalibur. The voiceover on the
commercial claims it lasts forever. I don't know if I buy
forever, but I admit the flashlight's pretty neat. Preacher's
explanation, though, is taking the fun out of it, and I'm surprised by my desire to have the Excalibur in my hand at
this very moment so I could coldcock him behind the ear
with it. When I get up to take a piss, I don't even think
Preacher notices. He's talking to himself more than to
Teddy or me.

When I return to the living room – needing a break
from Preacher, I took my time in the bathroom, actually
washed my hands as long as you're supposed to, a full
thirty seconds, and brushed my teeth, even flossed a little
– Preacher's gone. I look out the window and see his van
pulling out of the driveway. I sit down and wait for Teddy
to fill me in, but it doesn't appear he's going to on his own,
so I ask. "Where's Preacher going?"

"Emergency room," Teddy says. "After that, home. If
you have a family, that's where your Sunday afternoons
should be spent."

"Emergency room?" I say.

"He hurt his arm," Teddy says. "I was flipping around
during commercial, and on ESPN Classic they've got
arm-wrestling. Of course, Preacher starts in like he's an
authority, says it's not strength as much as quickness.
Starts crowing about his quick wrists, about what a great

high school baseball player he was, how as a boy he sprayed line drives all over northwestern Pennsylvania with his superhumanly quick hands. And then he starts hinting around he'd like to try me."

"What was he thinking?" I ask.

"He wasn't," Teddy says. "Obviously."

"So you broke his arm?"

"Broke? I don't know. Something popped."

"I didn't hear him yell."

"He's tough," Teddy says. "I'll give him that. Didn't whine at all. Just made faces, like when he's on his last few reps doing those curls of his. You ever watch him? Looks like he's filling his diaper."

"Should we follow him to the hospital?"

"He said no. Said he'd be fine. I think he was embarrassed. I think showing up at the hospital would be like rubbing it in."

"Wow," I say. "Poor Preacher."

"Yeah, right? Poor Preacher," Teddy says. "I was hoping he'd stick around all day."

When I next see Preacher, a couple weeks later at Titan's, his right arm's in a sling. He's doing dumbbell curls with his left.

"Preach," I say. "You should've waited for me. I'm probably more your speed."

"Waited for you?" Preacher says without looking at me. He has his eyes on Teddy, who's at the squat bar across the room. Preacher can see Teddy's face in the mirror. I don't know if Teddy's watching us or not.

"I'm saying you should've arm-wrestled me instead of Teddy."

"Arm-wrestle?" Preacher says, and then he turns to me and grins. "Right. Arm-wrestle."

If he had something more to say, he didn't say it. A talker like Preacher, I have to assume if there was more, he would've come out with it. Lookit, guys tangle. That's how guys are wired. Big guys, fit guys, especially. Guys start feeling good about themselves, and then what happens? Guys want to feel even better. You get two big, fit guys who want to feel better about themselves at the same time, in the same room, maybe a problem arises. But afterwards it blows over. Guys forget about it. It stays a problem only if guys let it stay a problem.

My living situation is I rent half a house. I spent years in beehive-like apartment complexes like the one Teddy lives in and told myself I didn't mind, but now that I'm living in a real house, I don't think I could ever go back.

The only drawback to where I am now is neighbors. Neighbors in and of themselves aren't problematic, of course, but a new neighbor who shares your property, who, in fact, lives in the other half of your house and doesn't pull his weight, is a problem. A neighbor who's supposed to split lawn mowing and snow shoveling duties with you but instead screws around all night and sleeps all day is a problem. This chore-splitting arrangement isn't informal or voluntary; it's in black and white, in the lease, and your old neighbor understood it just fine, but this new neighbor, this Blake, he doesn't get it. Not only that, he doesn't even say sorry, doesn't even say thank you. He takes for granted the clear driveway, the neat lawn. Maybe he thinks he's too good for these kinds of chores. Maybe he's just lazy. Or maybe he doesn't even notice whether the grass is tall or short, whether the driveway's clear or buried because he's oblivious. La-la land. This Blake, he wears his dyed black hair in a long ponytail, and he paints his fingernails black and sometimes wears black lipstick, and he sports the kind of earrings that fit inside and stretch out your earlobes, and no matter the season, no matter the weather, he wears this black leather jacket with black turtleneck and black jeans. It's hard to say what this Blake's deal is. Even though we're not allowed to have pets, I'm pretty sure it's his black cat who hangs around the grill with Teddy and me – he used to hang around with us, anyway; there's been no sign of the cat for a couple weeks; I fear for it – but do I squeal on this Blake to the landlord? Do I say to this Blake, "What the hell are you supposed to be, you freak? Are you a male witch? Are you in a punk band? Are you a Satan worshipper? What did you do to that poor cat that you're not even allowed to have in the first place?" No. I don't squeal, and I don't direct toward him any of these admittedly nosy, judgmental questions. What I do is, if I get his mail by accident, I put it in his mailbox. If he parks sloppily in the driveway so there's not enough room for my car, I park on the street. If he's listening to TV or music too loudly, I put on earphones, or I go for a walk.

The landlord's take on the lawn-mowing and snow-shoveling situation is that it isn't his problem. The lease says what it says. It's this Blake's and my responsibility to work it out. Working out details takes time and effort, though, probably more time and effort than just being the bigger man and shoveling the snow, cutting the grass.

This summer I've been mowing Sunday mornings before Teddy comes over. I'm showered and have the grill hot by the time he shows up, and there's that mown grass smell that helps me relax, and, I admit, because this Blake sleeps most of the day, I take some satisfaction in revving up the mower at nine or ten in the morning.

This past Sunday, though, a problem arises. When I pull the mower's starter cord, it doesn't start. Worse, the cord doesn't recoil, so I start tinkering around with it, thinking it should be an easy fix. I start loosening bolts and unscrewing screws and removing plates and covers and disconnecting connections, and before I know it, two hours have passed, and I have a couple blood blisters on my fingers, and the status of the lawnmower is that it's more apart now than together, more broken than fixed, and I've got no mind for small engines, and Teddy's scheduled to arrive within the half hour, and I haven't even cleaned or fired-up the grill.

What happens then is I get angry. The anger is at once rational and irrational, both righteous and unrighteous. If this Blake took his turn with lawn maintenance like he was supposed to, I probably still would've ended up with a busted mower somewhere along the line, but I'm convinced the point is more far-reaching than just here and now. The point is big-picture, last straw. The point is fair is fair. The point is justice for all.

I ring this Blake's front doorbell three times before he answers. The guy's fresh from the coffin. His pupils are dime-sized, and the whites are pencil eraser-pink. He's got a tattoo on his neck that wasn't there the last time I saw him. A row of stitches oozing blood. It's not that it looks real; it's that it looks worse than real.

"Hey," I say to this Blake, "sorry to wake you, but my mower's out of commission. You need to take on the grass cutting this week, OK? Maybe one of your friends has a mower? If not, there's that rental place downtown, behind the stadium, where you can get one for a couple hours. Anyway, from now on we alternate weeks like we're supposed to, OK? The past is the past, but starting today, OK?"

It's a sword that flashes out from behind this Blake's back as he jumps onto the porch, forcing me back onto the steps. At first he's just holding it in front of him vertically, but then he starts reciting gibberish in this deep, husky growl – it's not English he's speaking unless it's English backwards, like backward masking, like a spell of some sort, like he's looking to do harm to me not only physically but spiritually – and the sword starts spinning, faster and faster. What comes to mind is one of those little prop planes, those connecting flight planes. The ones that force you to ask yourself why you didn't go Greyhound. You've got a wing seat – everyone has a wing seat – and during takeoff, when the propellers start up, you watch how the three blades become one, and then eventually that one blade moves so fast that it's barely there; it blurs into almost nothing. That's this Blake and his sword.

This Blake's handled this sword before. He's practiced. He starts toward me slowly, little baby steps, and I run backwards as fast as I can toward the garage, but somehow he's gaining on me, and for a brief moment we're close enough that I can feel the breeze of the whirring blade, can smell hiscoffin breath. When we hit the driveway, though, he stops his pursuit, stills his sword above his head, directs more mumbo-jumbo words my way – his lids are fluttering so I can see that his eyeballs have rolled back in his head, like he's staring at his own brain – and then turns and sprints back through his door, back inside his hole.

My endorphins are raging, like they want out, like the sea they're swimming in is boiling. I'm slumped against the wall of the garage waiting for them to calm down, try-ing to get my heart rate under control, when Teddy pulls up. He unfolds himself out of his car and rushes over to me. "You OK, Elliott?"

I nod and push myself away from the wall, make myself stand straight. "Neighborly discord," I say.

"What happened to your leg?" Teddy asks, pointing to my thigh.

When I look down, I see that my shorts have been sliced only a couple inches to the left of my crotch. My skin's unbroken – there's no blood – but still, seeing it, it's a fight to stay standing.

"That weird dude who lives next to you?" Teddy asks, and he's halfway to this Blake's door before I even nod. When Teddy rings the bell, the door cracks open, and he pushes it in the rest of the way, and then he's inside.

I follow. The whole way to this Blake's door, I'm telling myself to hurry and get in there, and I'm telling myself to turn around and run.

Once inside, I see the sword on the floor, and I see that Teddy has this Blake pinned against a floor-to-ceiling bookcase. Teddy has him by the neck with one hand, and his other hand is cocked back, balled into a fist. After

Teddy's fist lands on this Blake's chin, Teddy lets him go, and this Blake falls to his knees. Then Teddy hits him in the ear with an open-hand slap that I imagine this Blake will never stop hearing.

Teddy takes a couple steps back then, and I take a couple steps up, so we're standing next to each other when this Blake pulls himself to his feet. When he raises his head and sees us, it's like he's surprised we're there, and what he says he has to say three times before we understand him.

"Sorry," he says. "Please don't report me."

"For the drugs you're obviously on? For assault with a deadly weapon? For being a worthless piece of trash?" Teddy says. "Be more specific."

"I just got out of prison this past year," this Blake says. He shuffles across the room to the couch and collapses. He's got one hand on his chin, the other on his ear. "This would screw me big-time. I'm sorry. Please."

"Not up to me, friend," Teddy says and then nods toward me. "That's the guy you need to apologize to."

"Elliott, right?" this Blake says to me. "Whatever I did to you, I'm sorry."

"You don't know what you did?" I say, pointing to my crotch.

"When I'm using, I have these episodes. I wig. You picked a bad time to come to my door."

"So it's my fault?" I say.

"No, like I said, I'm sorry." This Blake takes his hand away from his ear, then cringes and puts it back. "I'm scared here. I've been doing OK until just recently."

"So we do you a favor by keeping quiet, and then a week goes by, and we read in the paper that you've carved somebody up with your sword," Teddy says, walking over to it and picking it up.

"Saber," this Blake says. "Not a sword. A saber. Take it. It's worth thousands. What do I want with it?"

"Your call," Teddy says to me, handing me the saber.

"I really am sorry," this Blake says, and then he starts weeping. He doesn't try to hide it. He's out in the open with this weeping. A big vein pops up on his neck, bulging blue with this weeping.

"I don't want to see or hear you ever again," I say. I'm slapping my palm with the flat blade of the saber as I speak. "I want you to cut the grass for the rest of the summer, but I don't want to see or hear you do it. I just want short grass. When your lease is up, I want you gone, but I don't want to see or hear you moving out. I just want an empty house."

"Sure," this Blake says. "It'll be tricky, what you're asking, but that's my problem. Where to get a mower, when to mow, when to move, where to move. Figuring out those details is my problem."

"Let's go," Teddy says, and we both turn toward the door.

"You know, when I got out of prison last year, I was happy, of course, but you know what made me sad?" this Blake says. "Please," he says, "before you go. You know the first thing on the outside that depressed me? Riding away from the prison in my ex's car, I saw this sign on the highway: CORRECTION FACILITY AREA: DO NOT PICK UP HITCHHIKERS. That really bummed me out, right? To think I'm considered that dangerous. Dangerous enough to require signs. I'm thinking about that now because I'm feeling that same type of sadness. Like I've taken a step backwards. Are you sure I went after you with the saber?"

When this Blake is finished, I continue toward the door, but Teddy spins and flies back at him. This Blake sticks up one of his legs to protect himself, but Teddy sweeps it aside and lands two short, quick shots on the crown of this Blake's head. Like he's pounding a stake into the ground.

"He told you he didn't want to ever hear you again!" Teddy screams. "You didn't hear him say that? You're off to a bad start!" And then suddenly Teddy shoots past me out the door, and I follow, and then we're both standing in the sunshine, in the middle of the uncut front lawn, and Teddy's massaging his knuckles, asking me am I going to fire up the grill or what?

We go around back to the patio, and I don't know what to do with the saber, so I lean it next to the grill while I turn on the gas and strike the match. We both stand there watching the flames for a while, waiting for our breathing to even out. I'm telling myself we did what we had to do, that, in a big-picture sense, we did this Blake a favor, maybe gave him the wake-up call he needed, and I'm about to say out loud something along these lines when Teddy steps in front of me to close the lid of the grill and tells me to go ahead and shower, that he'll start lunch. A few minutes later, when I look out my bedroom window as I'm getting dressed, I see he's using the saber to flip our tuna steaks.

After I throw together a quick salad and Teddy brings the steaks in, we sit down in the living room with our food and switch on the TV only to discover that the Pirates game, our first choice, is getting rained out, so we turn to the Indians station where we find out Cleveland isn't going to get its game in either. Somehow Erie, smack-dab between the two cities, is enjoying sunshine while all around the heavens are opening. We switch over to the Weather Channel, and, sure enough, we see on the map that we're the only pocket of clear skies for hundreds of miles. It's raining not only south and west of us, but also east of us in Buffalo, north of us in Canada. Like Erie's being singled out, smiled down upon. Like we're being rewarded. Like everyone else is being punished.

Teddy and I settle on a movie neither of us recognize. We join it in-progress, and it looks like we've missed some important stuff, so it's hard to figure out who's doing what and why. Even after we're done eating, though, neither of us makes a move to switch the channel, so it looks like we're committed to it.

After a while I say something about one of the guys in the movie. I've never seen this actor before. I have a feeling he's not a real actor, that he's in the movie only because of his body, which is amazing. He's shirtless in every scene for good reason. The guy's sculpted out of granite. "Must be tough to find the time and energy to work out when you're always on the lam," I say. When Teddy doesn't answer, I look over to see he's fallen asleep. He's never done this before. I'm not sure why, but it unnerves me for some reason, him sleeping on my couch.

I pull myself out of the recliner and head out back to the patio to clean the grill. The saber's still out there, lying on the cement, and I think how stupid it was for Teddy and me to forget it out here. This Blake could've stolen it back. Anyone could've stolen it. Even if it's not worth the money this Blake says it's worth, a saber isn't something you want falling into the wrong hands.

I pick it up and turn to look at myself in the glass of the patio door. I strike a two-handed samurai pose and then get into a fencing pose, like I'm Zorro or a buccaneer. I'm not yet as lean and defined as Teddy and I want me to be, but I'm making progress. I'm getting there.

This Blake, his half of the house doesn't have a back patio like mine. The lawn runs right up to the door of his laundry room. My back's to it when I hear it fly open. When I turn, expecting to see this Blake, I instead see a woman, crying, holding her face with one hand. I don't know where this girl came from, if she was somewhere deep in this Blake's lair when Teddy and I were visiting with him or if she's arrived on the scene since, and I don't think I recognize her. This Blake gets plenty of visitors, but I always hear them arrive post-dusk and leave pre-dawn. The way she slams shut this Blake's back door, though, suggests she's a regular. The way she slams shut this Blake's back door suggests that it's a door she's slammed shut before, a door she's trying to convince herself she's slamming shut for the last time, and when she sees me, she

screams at me to mind my own business, as if I'm not
standing on my own patio. She passes directly in front of
me to get around the house, to the street, so I can see what
she's got is a nasty shiner, what's going to turn into one,
anyway, and when I ask if she's OK, instead of answering
me, she throws her head over her shoulder and says,
"That's Blake's sword. Not yours."

"It's not a sword," I call after her. What I should do, of
course, is follow her, offer her what she needs: an icepack,
a ride, my phone, a glass of water, advice. What I do
instead, though, is turn the other way, start toward this
Blake's door.

As I sheath the saber in the waistband of my shorts, I
feel my endorphins, whole schools of them, swimming in
sync, circling and swarming, like I imagine piranha must
circle and swarm. When I arrive at the door, I open it and
walk right in. I don't knock. Piranha don't knock.

I'm treading through this Blake's laundry room with
purpose, with what I imagine purpose must feel like, when
this Blake's cat, the one I'd come close to writing off, tears
out from behind the washing machine, runs over my feet,
ricochets off a pile of dirty sheets, and beelines for the hallway. This spooks me frozen, but when I hear this Blake
scream from somewhere deep in the house – "That you,
babe? Back for more?" – I know that's my cue, and my
feet are moving again even before I decide to move them,
and the saber's out of my shorts, leading the way toward
this Blake's voice before I can even ask myself what the
plan is. Like autopilot, like muscle memory. The thinking
part of me might as well be napping through rainouts
alongside Teddy. From here on in. For better or worse.
Out of my hands.

ROT AND SQUALOR

Fitz pops his whistle into his mouth but doesn't blow it. Not yet. He clinks it against his molars, tongues it up to his incisors, then works it down the other side of his jaw. Around the world. How Fitz thinks. Contemplation by mastication. In-season it's whistles; off-season it's pen caps and fingernails. Some nights, lost in TV, he'll gnaw the bottle cap of his beer doggedly enough to leave tooth-prints.

Fitz paces before his groggy team. Sprawled in the section of bleachers nearest the locker room, the boys wait silently for Fitz's instructions, work to avoid his glare. Fitz's dog, Worm, deceased as of last night, used to pull the same disappearing act with her eyes – her master's shame and disappointment is what she knew she'd see – after sprinkling on the carpet, dumping the kitchen garbage, chewing the headboard of Fitz's bed, or worse, escaping under the backyard fence and across busy Buffalo Road to the swamp, located kitty-corner to the parking lot of what used to be a Chi-Chi's. The swamp is where Worm was headed last night when she met a plumber's van in the eastbound lane. Fitz saw the whole thing, was trying to chase Worm down before she reached the road.

When the plumber got out of his van, Fitz could tell right away the guy knew what had happened. He was obviously shaken. Mournful even. Fitz ended up with the guy's business card before all was said and done. If there was ever anything Wayne Borst, Plumber could do for Fitz, he wanted to do it. If Worm had to be run over by someone, Fitz thought later that night, she could've done a lot worse than Wayne Borst. He seemed a good soul. A stand-up plumber.

Of course, what happened wasn't Wayne Borst's fault any more than it was Worm's. Wayne Borst was awake and sober, driving the speed limit, and had both eyes on the road. He wasn't talking on a cell phone or lighting a cigarette. As for Worm, her love of rot and squalor wasn't something she could resist or deny. It was instinctual. Couldn't be helped.

Fitz feels some guilt, of course. He could've saved Worm by turning her into a chained dog when she started digging under the fence, but with that type of salvation as the alternative, he can't quite convince himself he's any more at fault, any more of a culprit than Wayne or Worm. Could be there's such a thing as sinnerless sin. Transgressorless transgression. There are such things as victimless crimes, aren't there? Maybe there are. Name one.

On those occasions in her life when Worm had made it all the way to the swamp, she'd get her money's worth before Fitz came along, rubber boots on his feet and leash in hand, to escort her back home. She'd roll on her back in the filth, chase critters back into their holes, and feast on black mud and cattails while in-turn being devoured by clouds of mosquitoes. "The numero uno cause of heartworm," Fitz had tried to reason with her on more than one occasion as he hosed her off in the backyard. "You're eating death unto yourself, for hell's sake. Not to mention your breath stinks like a cesspit."

As Fitz watches his boys in the bleachers fumble with their sneaker laces, pick their acne, pull up and push down their socks, adjust their just-for-show Ace bandages, study the labels on their energy drinks, and spin basketballs between their knees, he wonders if a hose might do him any good in this setting. Bring this group back to life. His garden variety hose from home wouldn't be long enough to stretch from here in the gym all the way to the sinks in the locker room, but lack of water might not necessarily be a problem. He could still beat the boys with the hose.

Not really, of course. Thinking isn't the same as doing. Besides, even if he wanted to act on this notion, he couldn't because there's a witness-in-waiting lurking somewhere in the building. Kirk Gannon, Memorial's wrestling coach. Over the past few years, Gannon's taken great pleasure in the fact that the wrestling program's ascent has paralleled tough times for Fitz's teams. Back in the mid-nineties, when Fitz was regularly taking teams to the state tournament, Gannon had bemoaned how much attention the basketball program received, claimed he and his grapplers were being treated like second-class citizens. In those days, Gannon never looked in on Fitz's practices, never even attended games, but now that Fitz's boys are scrambling, he's a faithful spectator, and he brings the entire wrestling team with him to the games. Gannon's claim is they're there to show school spirit, but it's hard to take him seriously. The pack of them sit in the visitor's section, sweatshirt hoods pulled over their cauliflower ears and the backs of their thick necks, and howl loudly at their classmates' struggles. To keep up appearances of comradery, Gannon always seeks out Fitz in the faculty lounge the morning after a loss, grips his shoulder and offers strained, over-the-top condolences. Like someone Fitz loves is dying, or already dead, but this death is somehow something to fight back a smirk about.

Fitz knows Gannon's in the building this morning because the wrestling mats are out, and because when he

was at the urinal early this morning before any of his players had arrived, he'd heard whistling coming from one of
the stalls. When he glanced under the door on his way out,
he saw a huge pair of black wrestling shoes attached to a
pair of un-socked furry ankles. Gannon's a werewolf. A
sasquatch. When sporting his singlet, it looks like he's
wearing a custom-fitted bear pelt underneath.

So hose beatings of his players aren't an option this
morning for Fitz — of course they're not — but if they were,
he'd start with the cluster of players in the highest row.
They appear to be a bit more out of it than the others. Just
this side of comatose, they're intently occupied with nothing. They simply lean back on their elbows and aim heavy-
lidded stares past Fitz into the cold, musty air of the gym.

Fitz hasn't a clue what's going on in these twelve heads,
and he knows his not knowing is no small part of his problem. The injustice of 7:00 AM Saturday practices? The
beauty sleep they're missing? The cartoons? Their mom-
mies' pancakes? Could be the weather on their minds. The
first real snow of the season's falling outside. Maybe
they're wishing they were skiing, spinning doughnuts in
the parking lot with their parents' cars, navigating the slick
roads to the mall for some early bird Christmas shopping.
Or it might be girlfriends between their ears. Theirs, other
guys'. Prospectives, exes. Just as snow is the default
weather for Erie, Pennsylvania, it could be girls are the
default mind fodder for this group. Whatever the case, it
sure as hell isn't basketball they're mulling. Fitz has all
confidence this morning that not one of his forwards is
daydreaming about boxing out on the boards or hitting the
floor for loose balls; not one of his guards is fantasizing
about delivering crisp entry passes to the post or draining
open mid-range jumpers.

Fitz stops pacing to rub his temples and turn his back to
his audience like a comedian readying an impression. As
keenly as he feels it, he knows he can't let the boys see his
desperation. To steady himself, he pats the bulging hip

pockets of his baggy track pants like a gunfighter reminding himself of his holsters. This morning Fitz is packing props. There's an object lesson on the agenda.

Fitz didn't get a wink of sleep last night after what happened with Worm. He surfed channels until dawn. In the end, though, his persistence paid off. Watching the 5:00 AM edition of *Sports Center*, he heard one of the anchors quote George Orwell — "Sport is war minus the bullets" — and he was inspired. On his way to practice this morning, Fitz stopped in at the 24-hour Wal-Mart and bought a couple boxes of shotgun shells. They're what's in his pockets. His idea is to share with the boys Orwell's quote at the end of practice and then distribute the shells as commemorative keepsakes, to mark the occasion of the team's commitment, its vow to see the season through with integrity. Fitz imagines the boys taking the shells home, maybe putting them on their nightstands, finding ways to attach them to their key chains, or simply keeping them in their gym bags as good luck charms.

It's usually at least Winter Break before Fitz is forced in the direction of motivational gimmicks, but this squad is different. Not yet Thanksgiving, the season barely two weeks old, and they're already showing signs of surrender. They ghost-walk through drills; call out picks in bored, pipsqueak voices; and fake injury and illness in hopes of being excused from conditioning. These boys aren't only losing. They're losers. They're lost. Fitz knows if he doesn't get them back soon, they'll be gone for good.

Every year, the kids who suit up for Fitz are more distracted, more distant than the season before. This year's crop, you have to stand on your head and preach fire and brimstone to get their attention, and once you have it, you have to communicate with them like they're new to the planet. Then when the sun comes up the next day, you have to start all over again. This is what's most frustrated Fitz this season. These kids have no memory capacity, no ability to retain knowledge. A team of teenage amnesiacs.

Like any coach who's been at it as long as Fitz, he's all for frequently returning to fundamentals – he's a proponent of repetition, of back-to-basics – but, that said, it would be heartening now and then to see some evidence of progress. Fitz knows enough not to say "stupid" out loud, and he knows not to say "lazy" or "worthless" either, but how many credible explanations are there for mediocrity? Complacency? Half-assedness?

It's clear to Fitz now that he was in denial before the season started. The fact that the team's been so horrid out of the gate isn't all on the boys; Fitz has to be willing to take his fair share of the blame. He knows he's where the buck stops. During pre-season he'd told himself they had a chance in hell, told himself he'd seen worse. Wishing rather than thinking is what he was doing. He should've known better. You can't wish dead dogs alive; you have to let them lie. And you can't wish bad basketball teams good.

Fitz knows what's in the bleachers behind him, and he knows what's not there. There are no stars in the making on this team, no special players, no leaders. In terms of height, all twelve boys are right around average, within a couple inches of each other, and they're all a step slower than one another, and they're all right-handed with painfully weak left hands, and they're all nice guys with easygoing demeanors who like to please each other with goofy toilet humor, and they're not hungry, and they're not passionate. Last night against Lawrence Park, all of Fitz's guards were out-quicked, his entire frontcourt out-muscled. This is especially disturbing because Lawrence Park is projected to finish the season in the middle of the pack. Next up, this coming Tuesday, is Oil City, defending conference champs. Last year they beat Fitz's Memorial High squad by twenty-seven and were still pressing full-court with two minutes left in the game.

In terms of strategy, Fitz knows his options are limited with this team, and what he feels forced to do as a next step hurts his heart, his pride.

One of Fitz's most basic, most fervent convictions about the sport of basketball is that man-to-man is how defense is meant to be played. He believes it breeds aggressiveness, intimidation, and easy buckets at the other end. Problem is it's a defense for athletes, and he doesn't have any. Putting in a zone won't result in a win over Oil City on Tuesday, but it might save the boys, not to mention Fitz, from total humiliation. It might slow down the inevitable. So going zone feels to Fitz like the right move, but it also feels a lot like giving in, giving up.

What Fitz knows he can't do in starting this morning's practice is come out of the chute with a tirade about the 0-3 start or last night's particularly dreadful 19-point shellacking in which the team shot below fifty-percent from the line, was out-rebounded by a double-digit margin, and politely permitted Lawrence Park's twelfth man, a 5'5", 130-pound cherub look-a-like, to drain four uncontested three-point bombs in the waning minutes of the game. He'll have to remind the boys of these dire circumstances eventually, but he knows the importance of timing, knows that showing all his cards at the beginning of practice would diffuse tension, and that's the last thing he wants to do. A first-thing-in-the-morning dressing down is what the boys are half-expecting from Fitz – an excuse to mope is what they half-want from him – and if he gives them what they half-expect, what they half-want, they'll half-tune him out. Head games. For the next ninety minutes, Fitz wants last night's debacle to be the elephant in the gym.

Fitz finally turns, blows his whistle. He holds the note long and loud. He empties his lungs into it. In addressing his squad, Fitz's voice is even-keeled, measured. Professorial even. Fitz isn't only a Coach, after all; he's a teacher. Health and Phys. Ed. during the school year, Driver's Ed. in the summer, and no matter what some of his colleagues might think, Varsity Boys' Basketball isn't recess. There's pedagogy involved; there's psychology. There's even some of what Fitz is going to use to jump-start this morning's

practice. There's history. Basketball wasn't invented yesterday. Fitz needs his guys to understand he's not making this
stuff up, wants them to realize that both he and they are
parts of something larger than just here and now.

"We're done with man-to-man defense," Fitz says. "As
far as I can tell, we have no choice, seeing as how we have
no men." He hadn't planned this line. Just came out. Not
particularly witty but appropriately pointed. He pauses to
scan the boys' faces, gauge their ire. Nothing. As if he'd
just told them that turkey and pumpkin pie are rumored to
be on the menu for Thanksgiving dinner. That Lake Erie's
wet. That dogs howl, swamps stink, and plumbers have
dirty fingernails.

"So the word of the day is zone defense. Two words.
Two words of the day. The single two-word term of the
day." Fitz takes his hands off his hips, crosses his arms
across his chest, then drops them to hang loosely at his
sides for a moment before they creep back up to settle on
his waist. Twenty years of coaching, and no team's ever
turned him inside out like this. There are moments when
he feels like someone else, someone who doesn't know
anything, who doesn't know how to stand in front of a
group of kids in a manner commanding respect.

"We'll review the base 2-3 and the base 2-1-2," Fitz says,
"and then we'll see about putting in a few variations. OK?
You with me? First, though, a little background."

The zone defense was the brainchild of one Coach
Cameron Henderson, Fitz tells the boys. Henderson would
eventually make a name for himself at Marshall University
in West Virginia, but he came up with the zone concept early
in his career, when he was still zigzagging the Appalachians,
coaching small-town YMCA and church league teams. The
story goes that during one summer league game in which
Henderson was coaching, it got so hot in the gym that the
newly finished floor started to melt. They used real pinesap
in those days. People didn't believe in shortcuts back then,
didn't trust anything that seemed easy.

Fitz's tone here is nostalgic. Although he's not yet fifty, there's a wistfulness in his voice suggesting that he misses the days when the ball still had laces, guys shot their free throws underhand, and cheerleaders cheered rather than danced. The golden era of hoops.

So the pinesap, Fitz continues. It was a problem, impossibly sticky and slippery at the same time, like problems can be. Tough going for everyone, but especially for the defenders. Why especially the defenders? This is key. Offensive players know ahead of time where they're going; defensive players have to react. Playing man-to-man, if you get beat by a step, you have to possess the wherewithal and quickness to recover. In pinesap, it's difficult to possess quickness. It's difficult to possess wherewithal.

At halftime, Coach Cam and his boys hit the chalkboard – the players hung on every word out of their coach's mouth; young men in those days understood the importance of listening – and when the team took the floor after intermission, they fell back off their men to form a picket fence around the lane, offered their opponents nothing but long-range heaves.

The opposing coach complained, of course, got on the referee until the poor guy called time to check the rule book, but when the ref found nothing preventing Coach Cam's strategy, he told the other coach to shut his yap, see, that he wouldn't stand for any more bellyaching, see – this was how people talked back then – and he re-started the clock. Coach Cam's team went on to win. By the time his guys played their next game, the gym floor had dried, but the team stuck to their new defense.

The story doesn't end there, Fitz tells his guys. Most basketball people attribute the popularization and fine-tuning of the zone to Gene Johnson, who in the 30's coached high school ball in Kansas. His squads of farm boys shared the rock, set gritty picks and hit the boards like bullies, but they ran the floor as if headed uphill. Quicker teams from Wichita, Lawrence, and Topeka glided past Johnson's squad as if they were staked to the court like scarecrows. With the zone, though, Johnson found a way to play to his team's strengths, implemented a scheme that disguised slowness and emphasized the stationary tenacity rural Kansas is known for.

Fitz is interrupted at this point when one of the boys – Fitz isn't sure which; they're all equally careless and ham-fisted – loses the ball he was holding. There's some quiet tittering as it bounces lazily out of the bleachers toward Fitz, who catches it against his swelled pocket and holds it there, silently waiting for silence, before forging on.

"Of course, the story of zone defense doesn't end in Kansas, doesn't end with Coach Johnson. There are now sophisticated hybrid defenses. The diamond-and-one, the triangle-and-two. Match-up zones. You see them allowed even in the NBA now," Fitz says. "New chapters being written all the time. Fact is, we're going to write the next chapter here at Memorial. It has to be a collaborative effort, though. Collaborative meaning everyone in this gym has to pitch in. The key to zone is teamwork. You help, you rotate, you communicate. Each one of us has to re-commit to each other. Starting today. You with me? Yes? Are you or not? Let's go then! Stretch it out and then laps! Move!"

The boys limp to the middle of the floor where they form a clumsy sitting-circle around the team's three seniors. Fitz watches the guys for a few moments, can't decide if they look re-committed or not. Re-commitment's tough to gauge from a groin stretch, a sit-up.

Fitz turns his back to the boys, starts dribbling toward the north goal. When he comes to the top of the key, he shoots. Nothing but net. Had there been a three-point shot when he played high school ball, Fitz can't help but believe his respectable career numbers would have been spectacular. He knows a lot of ex-players around his age tell themselves the same thing, but does that necessarily mean he's wrong? One man's self-delusion is another's legitimate regret.

When the ball spins out of the net, it comes right back to Fitz like an obedient pet – this is what happens when perfect form results in perfect rotation – and he shoots again. He buries six in a row before clanging one too strong off the back of the iron. Fitz watches the ball carom to the corner of the gym, eventually coming to rest out-of-bounds against the rolled-up wrestling mats. Fitz knows the mats are a message. Gannon yanked them out of the equipment closet and put them on display at the crack of dawn to remind Fitz that he and his wrestlers are hosting a meet today, that Fitz and his gym rats need to be cleared out by 9:30 sharp.

Fitz grabs another ball from the rack and continues to shoot as the boys break their circle and begin taking laps. In seasons past, he'd always started off Saturday morning practices after losses with baseline-to-baseline sprints, but this team doesn't have the stomach for it. Literally. Last weekend, the morning after the first loss of the season, two kids threw up in the corner where the wrestling mats now sit, and a third lost it in the locker room. Naturally weak constitutions? A keg party in common the night before? Whatever the reason, during Fitz's playing days, even thinking back to teams he coached in the not too distant past, such a display of weakness would've been met with derision. The other guys on the team would've targeted the vomiters, labeled them as soft. In moderation, this kind of peer pressure can foster team unity, build bonds. The response of this year's squad, though, bewildered Fitz. They celebrated the guys who got sick. In the parking lot after practice, the infirm were still collecting high-fives and fist-bumps.

When the boys finish running, Fitz decides to forgo the usual ball drills. He needs to get directly to teaching if the new defense is going to be up and running by Tuesday night. He splits the boys into two squads. Five on seven. The Tylers and the Andrews versus the rest of the team. It's less confusing this way. This season, for the first time in his career, Fitz has had trouble keeping his players' names straight. Part of the problem is there are only nine names for the twelve boys. One each of Adam, Kai, Philip, Brandon, Malik, Wayne, and Kevin, but then there are two Tylers and three Andrews. The consequence is that the Tyler and Andrew squad doesn't get a sub. Their punishment for having unoriginal parents.

Fitz starts the Tylers and Andrews on defense. He maneuvers around each Tyler, each Andrew, showing the area each is responsible for. "If an offensive player comes into your zone, you're up in his jersey; once he leaves your area, though, you release him. You don't pursue. You trust your teammate to pick him up. If no man is in your zone, you rest up, right? You relax? No. The answer's no. You don't rest. You don't relax. Even if your zone is empty, you're still playing defense. Your arms are up, your knees are bent, and your head's on a swivel. With one eye you're following the ball, and with the other you're monitoring your boundaries. Border Patrol is who you are. Questions?" Fitz whips the ball to the point guard. "Let's work. Motion offense."

Just two passes and three dribbles later, the two-guard waltzes in from the wing to discover nothing but open space between himself and the hoop. He muffs the shot – this could be due in part to loneliness, he's that wide open – but he has plenty of time and room to get his own rebound, take the unnecessary dribble that Fitz is always telling his guys not to take, and lay the ball softly in the basket.

Fitz blows his whistle, throws his arms up in disgust, spins in place like an apoplectic ice skater, and tells the boys to run it again. The point guard holds onto the ball, though, because two of the guys on defense, one of the Tylers and one of the Andrews, aren't ready. They're still yapping about who was at fault for the breakdown. As their argument gains intensity, they step toward one another. Fitz tries to get their attention, but he might as well be screaming in Latin. He might as well be blowing a dog whistle.

When the boys' chins are about to touch, the Tyler bumps the Andrew in the chest with his shoulder, and Fitz hustles over to get between them, wraps one of his hands around the Tyler's arm, the other around the Andrew's, and squeezes both. "Trust," he says to the Tyler, his lips an inch from the kid's ear. "Teamwork," he says into the back of the Andrew's buzz cut.

"Again," Fitz tells the offense. "Motion."

A few passes later, the Andrew hits the deck. Fitz didn't see what put him there – a sucker shove, his own clumsiness – but when the kid regains his feet, he knocks back the Tyler with a two-handed face-push. The two players then take each other to the ground. They're almost gentle in their descent, more like tentative lovers than fighters. Their teammates don't move to break up the confrontation; rather, they back up, give their two fallen comrades space. They're more a cluster of peeping toms than an inciting mob.

Fitz is stunned. He rushes over with the intent to intervene but stops himself before moving in. They're not going to hurt each other. For better or worse, it's not in them. The Tyler, the one on top, looks the part – his cheeks are red, his nostrils flared – but he has no idea what he's doing. He appears to be trying for some sort of elaborate headlock instead of looking to drop fists and elbows. Like the match will be decided on style and originality. As for the Andrew, he looks close to weeping. He's flapping his limbs around like an upside-down turtle, and Fitz suspects that even if he could somehow manage to roll over, end up in the top position, his instincts would lean toward flight rather than fight.

Fitz has presided over some first-rate scraps in his career and knows that a good one can ignite a team. Teammate-on-teammate violence isn't something a coach should come out and condone – you always have to punish the participants in the name of sportsmanship and discipline – but at the same time, maybe you don't fall all over yourself to break up every beef right away. As long as the animosity doesn't linger, as long as it doesn't divide the team into factions and the participants don't sustain serious injuries, a spirited melee can serve as a wake-up call.

After only a few moments of watching the Andrew and the Tyler writhe around, though, Fitz knows nothing positive is going to come from this tussle. It's feeble and sloppy. Boring even. What's more, Fitz is beginning to wonder if the tiff might be about something off-court rather than on. Worse, it might be pointless, a by-product of immaturity and sleepiness. Two grumpy toddlers up past their bedtime tangling over a crayon. The longer Fitz watches, the more pitiful it seems.

Fitz's hands are in the pockets of his track pants before he decides to put them there, and he's screaming before choosing his words. "You guys want to battle? You want to war? Here you go!" Fitz winds up, stings the Tyler between his shoulder blades with a shotgun shell. "Bang!" Fitz screams. The Tyler winces, arches his back. "And here's one for you, Andy! Bang!" The shell bounces off the boy's throat, just to the left of his Adam's apple. He raises his hand demurely to cover the spot, like he's hiding a hickey.

The entire team is suddenly silent and still. The boys look confused. Fitz sympathizes. He's not entirely sure what's developed either. He knows he's jumped the gun, gone to Plan B when there was no Plan B. At no point had Fitz considered the possibility of peppering the boys with the shells like flushed waterfowl, but now that he's started down this road, he feels he has no choice but to follow through, whatever that might mean. The boys' eyes are popping. They're awake. Despite the glitch in execution, the momentary loss of composure, Fitz might've stumbled onto something worthwhile, and like any coach, he'd rather be lucky than good any day of the week.

"Got one with your name on it, Malik! Bang! Philip, get back here! Bang! Where do you think you're going, Wayne! Bang!"

As the boys are hit, they move off to the side to nurse
their welts as if this protocol had been agreed on before-
hand. The other boys, the not-yet-banged, remain in the
middle of the court. They look energized, peppy. There's
some nervous giggling developing, some juking and feint-
ing, even a hint of quiet trash-talk. Fitz sees one of the
boys, an Andrew, make a dash for the sidelines. The
shell's on its way to hitting the boy in stride when Kai, the
kid to the Andrew's immediate left, lunges to snatch it out
of the air like a superhero center-fielder. Fitz arches his
eyebrows, nods. Soft hands, good agility. And taking a bullet for a teammate. Impressive.

"Coach Fitzgerald! Freeze!"

The booming voice from the other side of the gym startles Fitz, but he recognizes it before turning.

"Boys!" Gannon says as he jogs over. "Everyone OK?
Anyone hurt? Enough for today, guys. Hit the showers."

"No one's going anywhere," Fitz says to his team, and
he turns to Gannon. "We've got another eighty minutes,
Kirk. Back off."

"Guys," Gannon says. He's still speaking loudly, but
now through his teeth. He's advanced to within inches of
Fitz, and even though it's the boys he's addressing, he's
looking Fitz in the eye as he speaks. "Do as I say, guys.
Your own safety."

Gannon bends to pick up one of the shells. He straight-
ens, turns it over in his hand, stashes it in one of the myr-
iad pockets on his snug cargo shorts. "Live ammo, Fitz?"
he says. "Have you lost it?"

The boys start across the floor toward the locker room.
They're mopey, hangdog, like they're the ones being lec-
tured.

"Whoa, guys. Hold up," Fitz says. "We're staying right
here. We're not done."

"You are done," Gannon says to Fitz. He's turned the
volume down now, is talking to Fitz in a barely audible
whisper. "You're over. I'm stepping in not just to save your

team from you. I'm saving you from you. What friends do." Gannon arches his unkempt eyebrows, nods in agreement with himself. "You know how screwed you are?"

This question catches Fitz off-guard. Its implications take a moment to sink in. "Kirk," he says. He places his arm on Gannon's shoulder, steers him away from the in-limbo players. "Aren't you overreacting here? I need to get through to them. Trying something unorthodox is all. Haven't I seen you in action? Your guys giving you piggy-back rides around the gym?"

"That's a legit conditioning technique, Fitz. It helps the chunky ones cut weight and builds the quads and lower back. Don't try turning this around. By the way, I participate in that drill only if one of my guys doesn't have a partner."

"I hear you. From an outsider's perspective it looks questionable, but you've got your legitimate reasons. There's method to your madness. Now can you give me the same benefit of the doubt here, the same professional courtesy?" Fitz leans in, gestures to Gannon's pocket. "Give me back the shell. I'm not going to throw any more. Point's been made. 'Sports is war minus the bullets.' George Orwell. It's literary. Let me get my practice in, and we'll be out of your hair in plenty of time. Good luck in today's meet, by the way."

"Sorry," Gannon says. "I have a responsibility. If I were to turn a blind eye to this sort of abuse and negligence, I'd be an accomplice. I'd be committing a sin of omission to complement your sin of commission. Not going to happen." Gannon presses his palms together flat like a praying child, rests them under his beard. "You need to clear out, and you need to let these boys get home. As for the meet this afternoon," Gannon says, "one thing I don't need is luck."

"Who do you think you are?" Fitz reaches out and grabs a handful of Gannon's t-shirt, inadvertently plucking a few of the man's chest hairs in the process. "Abuse?

Negligence? Omission? Give me my shell, and get the hell out of here."

Gannon's eyes open wide, and he nods over Fitz's shoulder. "Your guys are watching this. You're doubling your damage. What's more, you're asking for an ass-kicking."

When Fitz tightens his grip on Gannon's shirt and tugs, Gannon slides his right foot forward, lifts his knee to Fitz's groin, clears out Fitz's legs, and dumps him on his back. In his next motion, Gannon drops his shoulder on Fitz's chest, rolls him over onto his stomach, locks his right arm around Fitz's neck, grabs a handful of Fitz's hair with his left hand, and drives the coach's face into the floor.

Fitz feels his tongue rip, tastes blood. One of his teeth clatters loose, is flung to the back of his throat. He gags, stuck somewhere between inhale and exhale. The pain spreading from his groin into his stomach and up into his chest is squeezing his lungs, and his windpipe, clamped in the crook of Gannon's elbow, feels like a kinked garden hose.

Fitz tries to force himself to relax, concentrates on not passing out, not swallowing his tooth. He tries focusing on one pain at a time so as not to feel them all at once. Mouth, throat, chest, stomach, groin, then mouth again. Around the world. How Fitz thinks. And he listens. There's plenty to hear. Frantic voices, the chaotic squeaking of sneakers, and when Gannon's arm is finally pried loose from Fitz's voice box, his own loud, painful whelp.

Free now, but still flat on his back, Fitz gulps air, stares up into a ring of blurry faces haloed by the gym's fluorescent lights. That whine he just heard himself let loose sounded identical to Worm's bad dream noise, that high-pitched hiccup that originated deep in her belly during nightmares. The older she got, the more she had. Poor, haunted girl. He'd reach down from the bed to pet her awake from her tortured sleep. Sometimes she'd bare her teeth for an instant before recognizing his hand, but then, grateful to be back from wherever she'd been, she'd lick his fingers, sniff where she licked, then lick again.

Fitz rolls over with the help of some of his players, catches a glimpse of Gannon retreating to the locker room. The guy's doing neck rolls and arm windmills as he jogs backwards across the gym. Three warm-ups at once, like he's just beginning a workout. Or warm-downs, like mission accomplished, like he's just defended his belt.

Worm bared her teeth at Fitz last night. Her final gesture. Before Fitz assured Wayne Borst, Plumber that he could handle things on his own from here on out, before recrossing Buffalo road, getting a shovel from his garage, and then returning to cradle Worm to his chest, before carrying her across the parking lot to the swamp, Worm had rallied for a brief moment. When Fitz and Wayne had teamed up to drag what they thought to be her lifeless body onto the shoulder of the road, Worm's lip had curled, and when Fitz lightly touched her flank, told her her own name to let her know he was there, she'd snapped at him, clamped firmly onto two of his knuckles. He drew his hand back just for a second, but when he returned it to her, stroked the top of her head, she was gone.

In the moment, kneeling on the road's dark shoulder, Fitz couldn't think of one, and he couldn't think of one as he lay awake in front of the TV for the rest of night either. Even now, sitting under bright gym lights, staring at his own tooth in the middle of his own hand. Even now he can't. To bite the hand that feeds. Give him the rest of his life, Fitz still won't be able to come up with a worse ending than that.

SPOOKY ACTION AT A DISTANCE

Is this thing on? How do I know? Oh, I see. The red light. One-touch recording.

Is this thing on. Like I'm a flopping comedian, right, Dr. Samek? A lame joke about lame jokes. A joke within a joke. And here I sit in my wheelchair, literally lame, so a joke within a joke within a joke, right?

Seriously, though.

I'll do as you said, Dr. Samek, begin at the beginning, but I wish I knew if my mother has already gotten to you, if we're just wasting each other's time here.

I guess all I can do is ask you to hear me out, to keep an open mind. If I'm to find a way to face the truth of what's ahead, I have to find someone to help me face the truth of what's already been. Does this sound to you like deluded thinking, Dr. Samek? Do I sound like a crazy person? If not, maybe you can help me. Maybe this isn't a waste of time.

The truth begins and ends with Ishmaael − my twin? my big brother? my host organism? − who was born in Kazakhstan thirty years ago, six or seven years before me.

I have yet to establish precisely my true age as I distrust both the paper trail and my own fuzzy memories. My distrust isn't misplaced, is it? Aren't paperwork and memory both susceptible to tampering? To manipulation?

I know, Dr. Samek, what my mother says about all this. She says I'm delusional, says Ishmaael was born in the States like me, says we were born within minutes of each other, months after she left Kazakhstan. She won't give an inch on any of this. She knows her whole story will unravel if she compromises even one detail. What's sad is she and I love each other — Ishmaael's suicide has brought us even closer, I think — but we have this story between us.

But I'm in the process of piecing together the truth. I now know, for instance, that, in the beginning, Ish was a normal Kazakh boy. He walked on time, talked on time, but just before he was to start school, he began suffering chronic bellyaches, and his stomach started to bulge. Before long his belly was fully distended, a swelling half-balloon that forced him into his father's shirts. Eventually he stopped leaving the house, partly due to the pain, partly due to the other kids — they'd point at his stomach and call him 'Mommy,' ask him why he liked to eat soccer balls — and when he lay down at night, he began to have trouble breathing. As his condition worsened, he had trouble keeping down food. Even as the rest of him wasted away, though, his belly kept growing.

An upsetting story, right, Dr. Samek? Not just for Ish, of course. Imagine his parents. How confused and desperate they must've been. Imagine their anxiety as they listened to their neighbors' theories. 'The boy has rickets.' 'The boy must've eaten some unwashed fruit.' 'The boy was bitten in the belly by a bat.' 'The boy's actually a girl.' 'The boy's parents have displeased Allah.'

Fervent prayers were offered by all who knew him, but his belly wouldn't flatten.

Unbelievable. What timing. Excuse me, Dr. Samek.

Sorry about the interruption, Dr. Samek. Mrs. Jagow, my nurse, poked her head in to ask if I'd mind an earlier than usual bath. She's supposed to knock. I've reminded her of this on multiple occasions, have even had my mother speak to her, but it evidently hasn't sunk in. I don't think she's forgetful; I think she's nosy. She's always trying to sneak a peek at what I'm watching on TV, what website I'm on. Now, of course, she's dying to know what I'm up to with this recorder, but she won't just come out and ask. Instead she'll press her ear up against my door, or she'll pump my mother for info.

You ever see *One Flew Over the Cuckoo's Nest,* Dr. Samek? A must-see for people in your field, right? Remember Nurse Ratched?

Jagow's bathing me is a necessary evil. My trade-off for good hygiene is having the sow wheeze and grunt over me once a day. I would've asked her to hold off until I was finished recording, but she said she needed to leave early today to stalk someone or arrange a hit on her husband or torture stray cats with an electric prod. I forget the specifics. At any rate, I'm back. Squeaky clean, a new man. Jagow's sponge leaves unscrubbed not one nook, not one cranny.

Oh hell. Am I recording over what I did before my bath? Oh, no, I'm OK. I see. Before is on here as '001'. Now is '002'.

Before I continue, I'll confess, Dr. Samek, that I'm a little wary of this whole process. This recording thing. The logistics. How exactly do you see it working? I give the recorder back to you at our next session, and then what? You listen to it on your own at a later time, take notes? It's like a tool for you? To give you a better handle on what you're up against? Or do we listen to it together? Like if we have a lull in our session, we'll use the recording to get back on track? Only one face-to-face meeting under our belts, and we've already had our share of lulls, right? Did the lulls worry you? Is that what's behind this?

The lulls were my fault, Dr. Samek. I've been tired. Sleeping is a challenge lately. Plus, meeting new people is difficult for me. I can seem standoffish. I've had some bad experiences. People have fainted at the sight of me, Dr. Samek. Not entirely surprising, right? Let's be honest.

Anyway, when it comes down to it, I suppose the logistics don't matter much because I'm going to feel uncomfortable no matter what. If you listen to this by yourself, it'll bug me knowing I'm not there to clarify what I meant if I end up saying anything requiring clarification. What could I possibly say that wouldn't require clarification? On the other hand, if I team up with you to eavesdrop on myself, that'll feel creepy. Where will I look as I listen to myself? At the recorder? At the floor? At your face? You'll have to bite the bullet and watch me, right? To gauge my reactions?

By the way, Dr. Samek, the worst thing you could do is lie about my appearance, tell me it's not a problem for you. I'm a horror. It's a given. What did you tell the other shrinks after our appointment? You probably have a shrink bar you go to, right? You and your colleagues sit around sipping scotch, smoking pipes, comparing war stories. 'You think I'm exaggerating? I wish I had a picture.' I bet you said something like that. Please don't feel bad. In a perfect world, my face wouldn't be a problem for my psychiatrist because he of all people should be able to see behind the face, beyond the face, but this world's not perfect. Is that your fault, Dr. Samek? The imperfection of this world? Tell you what. You can take a picture of me next time. Your cronies at the shrink bar will get a kick out of it. I'll try to look extra gory. I'll drool, squint, and grimace. I'll wear a tie.

I'm being shitty. I'm sorry. I've gotten off-track here. I admit I'm sensitive about my appearance. It's not about vanity, though, it's about how my appearance keeps people from listening. When I speak, people don't hear what I'm saying. I believe I can come off as bright and witty given the right conditions, but to most people, I might as well meow or bark. I might as well growl or hiss. They can't use their ears on me because they're too busy using their eyes. Even my mother sometimes. Even Ish when he was alive. The flesh and blood fact of me freaks out even my own flesh and blood.

Were you listening to me in our face-to-face session, Dr. Samek? It looked like you were, but as a shrink, you're probably a champ at looking like you're listening when you're not.

Which of my features horrifies you most, Dr. Samek? My pancake nose? My caved-in forehead? What I look like is a melting snowman, right? How about my stray eye? My rabbit eye. No farmer's going to sneak up on me in the radish patch, split my head with a hoe. At least not on my left. Maybe for you, though, it's my fingers. They're nice, right? Long and slender, immaculate nails – Jagow's skilled with a file – and just the right number of hairs below each knuckle. Perfect. Considering the rest of me, that's what makes them so disturbing, right? They don't seem like they should belong to me.

Is this unfair, Dr. Samek? Speculating like this? Putting words in your mouth, thoughts in your head? Have I been bullying? Sorry.

I'm not doing this right, am I? You said it would be impossible for me to do it wrong, but I think wrong is always, in all cases, an all-too-likely possibility.

I feel now like what I should do is erase everything and start over, but you said the only rule for this assignment is no erasing. So I guess I won't erase, but, really, how would you know? I could've already started over. This could be the fifteenth version. You wouldn't know, but I'd know, right? You're counting on my conscience. The honor system.

I think we need a break, Dr. Samek. I need to gather myself, give myself an attitude adjustment.

Back again, Dr. Samek. Do you hear the sheepishness
in my voice? Once more, I'm sorry. I've watched some
TV, had some supper. Back-to-back Baywatch reruns and
Kraft dinner. My mother's out tonight, but, lucky for me,
Jagow's a whiz in the kitchen. Anyway, the grumpy bug
has crawled out of my ass. That's Jagow's expression.
When I snap at her, she leaves the room, threatening to
return when the grumpy bug crawls out of my ass. In the
moment, the phrase can really piss me off, but out of the
moment, like now, I see how it could be considered vul-
garly amusing. Like *Baywatch*, right?

Anyway, so back to it. Back to Ish. Back to the truth.

His condition finally progresses to the point his parents
are worried they're losing him. Their only child. Despite
the disapproval of their neighbors and family, they see no
choice but to summon a doctor from the city. If calling a
doctor from Almaty is a sin, if it reflects lack of faith,
they're sorry, but wouldn't it also be a sin to pretend to
have faith they don't have? Besides, isn't putting the life of
their son in a stranger's hands a kind of faith?

I'm trying here to put myself into the minds of Ish's
parents. I've been accused by my mother and others of
hyperextending my imagination, of confusing speculation
with fact, but I can only play the hand I've been dealt. I've
been forced to discover the truth of Ish's story, of my own
story, independently because those in the know aren't talking other than to lie, to try to convince me I'm inventing
this tragedy to avoid dealing with the real tragedy that I
need to face. They tell me I've adopted my story as a cop-
ing strategy, a way to put off coming to terms with Ish's
suicide.

They're wrong, Dr. Samek. When I heard the doctor
on TV tell the story of the Kazakh fetus-in-fetu case, I
knew without a doubt that I was listening to my own story.
Each detail kick-started long buried memories and brought
me, simultaneously, great relief and anxiety. Imagine yourself in my shoes. Wouldn't you be able to recognize your

own life story, even if you heard it told for the first time by a stranger on TV?

I admit my mother's story is compelling, even feasible, but compelling isn't the same as true; feasible isn't the same as true. After careful consideration, I'm convinced that, in telling my story, I'm neither inventing nor borrowing; rather, I'm reconstructing. 'But it's something you heard on TV!' my mother pleads, as if that's somehow relevant. Admittedly, I watch a lot of TV. My lot in life, I think that's understandable. But in this case, I wasn't watching the Sci-Fi Channel, Dr. Samek. I wasn't watching Comedy Central. I was watching the Discovery Channel, and I've verified much of what I heard and saw through web research.

What most convinces me, though, isn't my research, isn't the way I've been able to connect fact to fact. What most convinces me is that every time I tell the story, to myself or someone else, I become more sure of its truth. The story helps me remember itself more clearly. It gets truer in each telling. Are there unanswered questions? Are there holes? Of course. And I'm working to answer these questions, fill these holes. But what does it mean to believe a story without accepting its built-in mysteries? Nothing. That kind of belief means nothing.

I understand your skepticism, Dr. Samek, but the truth isn't always easy to believe; the truth isn't always likely. Conroy, the doctor interviewed on the Discovery Channel program, is the same man who, I believe, was summoned nearly twenty-five years ago by Ish's parents to examine their son's swollen belly, the same doctor who examined Ishmaael and in no time at all announced loudly, confidently, his diagnosis. His dead wrong diagnosis. 'The boy has a tumor,' he said. To learn more about the nature of the tumor, he insisted on having Ish transported back to Almaty for tests. 'There are questions we need answers to, and to get these answers we need to get inside the boy,' the good doctor told Ish's parents. 'Is it cancerous? Operable?

Is there more than one? These are some of the issues. Poking and pressing from the outside can only tell you so much.'

You know what comes next, don't you, Dr. Samek? When Dr. Conroy and his team opened Ish, it wasn't a tumor they saw. It wasn't a what at all. Or, at least, it wasn't only a what. It was at least part who. It was me.

Do you know what a fetus-in-fetu twin is, Dr. Samek? When my mother and whoever else had their strategy pow-wow with you, did they educate you about my so-called delusions?

I memorized the basic definition, mouthed the words to myself like a mantra for days. Even now it's comforting. The repetition of the truth of what I am:

'A fetus-in-fetu is an encapsulated, pedunculated, malformed monozygotic, monochorionic, diamniotic, parasitic twin included in a host twin. Characteristically the fetus-in-fetu complex will be composed of a fibrous membrane, equivalent to the chorioamniotic complex, that contains some fluid, equivalent to the amniotic fluid, and a fetus suspended by a cord or pedicle.'

Not bad, right? Do you suspect that I read it instead of reciting it? Believe me, I didn't. You have my word. The honor system.

Fetus-in-fetu twins are not as rare as you might think, Dr. Samek. Fifteen percent of all living people had a twin at some point in their embryonic development, a twin who faded away, dissolved or, in some cases, was delivered stillborn. What distinguishes me from your twin if you had one is my perseverance, my stick-to-it-iveness. I'm the first fetus-in-fetu to gulp air.

If my story got out, I could be the poster-child for both pro-life and pro-choice groups. I could be the poster-child for anything. For everything. If only I were more photogenic, right, Dr. Samek?

Dr. Conroy is dead, Dr. Samek, and this fact greatly complicates things. If he were alive, he could shed some light on this situation. On the TV program, he claims that the fetus-in-fetu, while relatively well-developed, wasn't delivered alive. Couldn't have been. Its arteries were connected to its brother's aorta. It didn't have its own heart. In the interview, he goes as far as to call the fetus-in-fetu a parasite. Like a barnacle, a tapeworm, a fungus. Why did he tell these lies? I'd like to be able to ask him this.

What do you think so far, Dr. Samek? Are you siding with those who think my story is a by-product of denial? Then answer me this: What am I avoiding by believing what I believe? I'm not in denial about Ishmael's death. I'm not in denial about my disabilities and appearance. I'm not seeking to avoid these tragedies; I take them on, head-on, every day. You don't know the half of what I'm taking on, Dr. Samek. You don't know because I haven't yet told you.

Sorry about the dead air at the end of the last recording, Dr. Samek. I paused, deciding where to go next, and the pause turned into a nap. Like I said, I've had trouble sleeping at night.

If you listen closely to the dead air, you can hear me mumbling between snores. I can't quite make out what I was saying. Can you? I'm curious. Maybe there's a way to enhance the recording?

I'd love to see your notes at this point, Dr. Samek. I imagine your questions are starting to pile up. What do I believe my mother's motivation is for denying me the truth? Do I think that my mother thinks she's acting in my best interest? Do I think that she thinks she's protecting me? Why did Ish go along with her story even to the end? Do I think the going along is what wore him out finally?

Do you think your pile of questions is higher than mine, Dr. Samek?

I won't pretend to have answers worked out for every question, but I think I've solved some of them. Why did

Ish go along with my mother's story? Consider this: You're an eight year-old boy who's just given birth to your kid brother. Aren't you starving for a lie to latch onto? Aren't you starving to believe it was all a nightmare?

Don't you think I've been tempted to give in myself, Dr. Samek? To trade my story for my mother's? It would be a great relief if I could go back to believing I don't have a father back in Kazakhstan, a father who abandoned us when word of me reached him back at the village where he'd waited, a coward. It would be a relief to believe this father didn't forward a message to my mother saying that she and her two sons would never be welcomed back home. It would be a relief to believe this father didn't read me as a sign that his wife had shared Satan's bed. It would be a relief to believe this father didn't say that if he ever again saw us, any of us, he'd kill us.

It would be a relief to believe my mother's claims that she's never been married, that Ishmaael's and my father is an American doctor who lives in New Jersey and sends us money, that he worked for a short time in Kazakhstan as a missionary doctor, that he had a fling with my mother and then brought her, pregnant, to America to set up a life for her, even if separate from his.

As evidence of this American father, my mother's produced checks signed by a Dr. Graham Reese. She thinks these should convince me. I'm asked to believe I was as normal as Ish when we came out of her, one after the other, in a Chicago hospital. She thinks a photo album full of snapshots of perfect twin babies is supposed to convince me of this. I'm asked to accept that my body and face are the result of a car accident that occurred on the Kennedy Expressway when I was a toddler. She shows me her own scars, one above her left eyebrow where her head supposedly caromed off the steering wheel. I'm asked to accept that I'm the byproduct of an improperly installed car seat, a flight through an open rear window, and a series of complex surgeries, some performed by colleagues of my father.

What my mother tells me, what I'm sure she's told you, is that I need to get to the root of why I reject her version of my life, why I cling to my own. She's read just enough pop psychology to be dangerous. She talks to me of survivor guilt, of owning my grief. This is why she's set me up with you. She thinks you're the one who can help me come to terms with Ish's death. Like me, she wants you to be the one.

I need another break, Dr. Samek. Where we go next is important. I don't want my mouth to get ahead of my brain.

Do you like beer, Dr. Samek? I like beer. Some nights after Mrs. Jagow's gone, I tell my mother to go buy me a six-pack – I like Guinness in the winter, Corona in the summer – and she does. It's bad for me – who's it good for? – but could you say 'no'? The half-human in the wheelchair asks you for beer, you bring him beer. Despite his delicate system you bring him beer. You fill up his sports bottle – if you get sneaky and try to water it down, he'll know, and he'll be pissed – and you set it in his lap. He sucks his straw, gets a bellyache, pisses and farts. You fill his bottle again when he asks, and then he falls asleep. What's the harm?

Anyway, I'm into some beer right now – so much for the thinking I had to do, right? – so I'm warning you I might not last too long. I'm close to calling it a day.

There's nothing on TV, Dr. Samek. I'm surfing through all trash right now. When Ish and I were growing up, we had fewer channels, but we could always find something to watch. Isn't that strange?

Growing up, TV was what Ish and I had in common. Most of the time we spent in the same room was because of TV. When Ish got home from school, I'd already be done with my tutors, parked beside the green recliner, waiting for him to crash on the couch. We'd be there through supper until my mother shooed us away to do homework –

she'd watch the evening news during this break – and then we'd return to our spots for prime time. Ish and I didn't talk much in the TV room, but we each appreciated the fact of each other's presence. The whole idea behind the sitcom laugh track, right?

Ish's favorite show was *The Incredible Hulk*. Remember that show? The live action series starring Bill Bixby? At the beginning of each episode, you'd see Bixby's character walking away from his own tombstone. He'd had to fake his own death to buy himself some time, to figure out how to beat the monster he'd become. He roamed from town to town, and when a bad guy pissed him off, his eyes would turn green. The camera would leave him for a split second, usually to gauge the expression on the face of whoever it was who'd angered him, and when the camera got back to Bixby, he wasn't Bixby anymore; he was Lou Ferrigno, that deaf body builder, covered with green make-up. The change was the climax of every episode. It's why Ish loved the show. He'd sit up in anticipation when Bixby's eyes turned green, and after the transformation, at the next commercial break, he'd re-enact it. I like to think at least part of the reason he did this was because he knew how funny I thought it was. 'Don't make me angry,' he'd say as he messed up his hair and packed throw pillows under his shirt. 'You wouldn't like me when I'm angry.' Then he'd jump up and down on the couch and roar like a psychotic. It was hilarious. He'd carry on until our mother yelled for him to stop.

I liked the show, too, until one day I saw another Bill Bixby show called *The Courtship of Eddie's Father*. Does that show ring a bell? Bixby's a single father of this dark-haired, freckled, Bobby Brady look-alike. It was an OK show, but it ruined *The Hulk* for me. Now when I saw Bixby walking away from his own tombstone at the beginning of *The Hulk*, I couldn't help but think of his kid from the other show. Bixby's death wouldn't have been fake to his son. Bixby probably thought he was doing Eddie a favor by going away, but who says Eddie couldn't have helped his dad with the Hulk thing? Who says Eddie couldn't have learned to love the Hulk as much as he loved Bixby? If Bixby spared Eddie any pain by leaving, he also caused him pain.

Anyway, this is what turned me off The Hulk. I couldn't explain it to Ish, of course. I knew it was nonsensical. So I just started saying The Hulk was boring. That every episode was the same. That it wasn't believable.

One night when we were watching the show, Ish left the room during a commercial, so I wheeled to the couch, got the remote, and turned the channel. When he returned he was furious and grabbed the remote back. I yelled for my mother, who came into the room and, after hearing both sides, announced that the TV would be turned off for the rest of the night. Ish stood to storm out of the room and tossed the remote in my direction. It hit me in the mouth, bloodied my lip. When my mother saw my blood, she slapped Ish, and then she cried – I was crying already – and Ish, not crying, just looked back and forth at us, trying to figure out who he was angrier at, before leaving the room.

I remembered this at Ish's funeral. The bloody lip, the slap, the crying. Strange thing is it made me feel a little better. Or maybe you don't think that's strange at all, Dr. Samek. You've got the human mind all figured out, right? Why it does what it does, why it goes where it goes? The Hulk could've used someone like you, Dr. Samek. Someone with your expert insight, your professional knowledge. Someone with a prescription pad who could've set him up with some Xanex.

You know what I wish, Dr. Samek? Do you get mistaken for a wish-granter by some of your patients? A genie? You know what I wish was on TV right now? I wish on TV right now there was a movie of my life. I wish it was just now beginning because I feel the need to see Scene One, the one set in the operating room where they pull me out of Ish.

Maybe I'm wrong, though. Maybe that's not the opening scene. Maybe the movie starts way before that. Pre-me. Even pre-Ish. Even pre-Ish's mother, pre-Ish's father. A movie about a creature like me should go back even further than that, right? Pre-people. The first stages of everything. Back to when there were just pre-historic monsters and God. Evolutionary times. Birds shedding scales; dinosaurs sprouting wings; new, first-of-their-kind things scurrying in and out of the dark, bubbling pools; God holding His breath over every hatching egg.

Maybe He still holds his breath, right? When they pulled me out of Ish, was God holding His breath then? How long can He hold His breath? Is He still holding it? Maybe He held it too long and passed out? Or worse than passed out. Ish in his noose. That's as good an explanation as any other I've been able to come up with. God worse than passed out.

Good morning, Dr. Samek. Correction. Good afternoon.

I slept heavily last night. I don't remember waking up at all. That's rare for me. I remember dreaming, though. When I drink beer – even sometimes when I don't drink beer – I've been having this one particular dream. You shrinks live for this stuff, right?

I'm a fetus again, back inside Ish. It's one of those undreamlike dreams. It's not what happens in the dream that takes me by surprise; it's the waking up that's shocking. The dream's so real. The position, the climate, the sound. Upside-down, warm and wet, gurgling. In the dream, I'm not thinking, I'm just being. Is it that I'm inside the thick, yolky bubble, or is it that I myself am the thick, yolky bubble? Yes and yes.

Is this a common dream, Dr. Samek? The fetus dream? Is it textbook like the flying dream? The naked in public dream? The driving without brakes dream?

Then there's another I keep having. I don't have it as

much as the fetus dream, but almost as much. In this one my mother lets go of her story, admits everything to me, and tells me my father was wrong, that I'm not a curse, that I'm not nonsense. She tells me I'm a miracle, and that from here on in every day will be my birthday, and then she bows to hug me, and crawls into my lap, and I hold her like she's the child. What she says about every day being my birthday makes me feel like I've always been, like I'm beginningless, like God, but this doesn't make me unafraid, Dr. Samek. It makes me the opposite of unafraid.

A few months back, when I was trying to figure out how to confront my mother, I thought about leading with these two dreams. Telling her about them. I thought maybe they would crack her, that she'd spill her guts after hearing them. Psychological and emotional warfare, right? I finally decided to go in a different direction, though. I decided I needed something more tangible than a dream. I wanted her to understand in clear, concrete terms what I knew.

I came up with Matryoshka dolls. You know what I'm talking about? A large doll opens to reveal a smaller doll, that smaller doll opens to reveal an even smaller doll, that even smaller doll opens to reveal a still tinier doll, etc. For my mother's birthday, I ordered a hand-painted set online, and after she unwrapped them, I told her to take them apart and put them in my lap. I then touched the smallest doll and said, 'This one is me.' Then I touched the medium doll and said, 'This one is Ishmaael.' Finally, I rested my hand on the largest doll. 'This one is you,' I said. 'Do you see? It's too late for Ish but not for us.'

The way she looked at me told me she understood, told me she wanted to start living with me in the truth. She got out of her chair and knelt in front of me, and she touched my face like she used to when I was a kid, but the words she said didn't match what I thought I was seeing. She said, 'You're upset about your brother. You need help. I'll get you help.'

I thought then what I was trying to tell my mother through the Matryoshka dolls was the whole truth, Dr. Samek, but now I don't. I don't think I'm the smallest doll anymore.

We're getting to it now, Dr. Samek.

Do you know anything about Einstein? His idea of spooky action at a distance? When I was a kid, one of my tutors told me about it. Einstein was thinking physics, of course – photons or electrons or whatever-trons; I don't remember the science part of it – but the phrase was borrowed by non-scientific types and applied to twins, used to describe that inexplicable connection some twins seem to have with each other. Do you know what I'm talking about? At the exact moment a man suffers a massive heart attack in London, his twin experiences crushing chest pain in Indianapolis. A golfer scores a hole in one in Corpus Christi, and his twin in Providence experiences an adrenaline rush. A woman in Vancouver makes love, and her twin, sleeping alone in Tokyo, awakens to an orgasm.

Did I have this type of connection with Ish, Dr. Samek? Do I still, death be damned? How spooky can this action get? How much distance can it cover?

I sort my memories of Ish, now through the filter of truth, and see hints he dropped, signs I missed. There were innumerable anxious looks, and he had a habit of trailing off in conversation, of not finishing sentences, completing thoughts. Perhaps that's part of what I'm doing now. Carrying to term his aborted sentences and thoughts.

At times the silence between Ish and me seemed to be leading somewhere. I've heard my mother tell people that we weren't close, Ish and I, but I wonder how she comes to this conclusion. I wonder if she believes it. It's true that when we were kids he was embarrassed of me, that after we were grown and he'd moved out, she'd have to remind him to visit, but were these signs of distance between us, or were these signs of guilt on his part? What there was separating us, I don't think it was anything the truth wouldn't have been able to dissolve.

The fetus dream I'm having, Dr. Samek, I suspect it's not my dream. I suspect it's being dreamed inside of me, that Ish is dreaming this dream inside of me. Matryoshka dolls in chaos. The smallest doll opens up to reveal a still smaller doll, or is it somehow the larger doll it contains? Can the larger doll and the smaller doll contain each other, Dr. Samek? This is part of what I need help with.

Church people think they have answers, right? If you don't work out, maybe this will be my next move. They come door-to-door through our neighborhood, and my mother always invites them in to meet me. She summons me, I roll myself into the living room, and a lot of them, you can tell, are on the verge of losing what they think is their faith right then and there. The answers they thought they had? After seeing me, they can't even remember the questions. The fainter I mentioned before? A Baptist. My mom and I just smile. It's not an innocent thing we do.

This one lady who came the week after Ish's suicide, though, stood her ground. I can't remember her denomination. For all I know, she could've been on the same team as the fainter. At any rate, I didn't faze her. She looked me in the face as she smiled, handed us her tracts, and went through them with us like I imagine she does with everyone. Then she let us know that she'd heard we'd experienced the loss of a loved one, and she asked if she could pray with us.

'We're Muslim,' my mother said, even though we're not, not really. Her not anymore, and me not ever.

'Prayer's prayer,' the woman said, and she smiled and launched into it. It wasn't what she said in her prayer that struck me, though − I forget what she prayed − but what she said right before she left. 'Friends,' she said, 'we may attribute miracles to God, but not nonsense.' She said it like she'd been saving it, like everything she'd said up to that point, prayer included, had been prelude.

She was referring specifically to the nonsense of Ish's death, of course, but she was also in some sense talking about me, right? My life? Not only what it's been but what it's to be?

Miracle? Nonsense? Is there a difference, Dr. Samek? Truth?

As if God's not dead. As if He is.

The doll analogy can only take us so far, right, Dr. Samek? It's too broadly applicable, right? Who isn't like a Matryoshka doll? Someone in your line of work, I'm sure I'm not telling you anything new. Who doesn't contain multitudes?

Bath time again, Dr. Samek. Jagow's making preparations as I speak. Hear the water running? Hear her filing her teeth?

I don't think I've done a good job here, Dr. Samek. I'm not satisfied with how I've laid things out for you. I don't think your hearing this would be productive. After my bath, I think I'm going to erase everything. Start over. So much for the honor system.

So I guess I'm not talking to you now. Or I am talking to you, but I'm talking to you knowing you'll never hear this. Is this what prayer feels like?

Jagow's tuneless whistling. Hear her? Like a brain-damaged, tone-deaf bird. She can't wait to sink her talons into me. Hear her squawking? A mother pterodactyl. I wouldn't be surprised if she had a few scales on her somewhere. The woman evolution left behind. Like we were saying before, right? Back when God started to hold His breath. With screeching like that, maybe He also had to cover His ears.

We'll get this right, Dr. Samek. We'll start over and get this right. We'll keep starting over until we get this right.